hWild
hunters

STUART R BROGAN

Published by Horrific Tales Publishing 2021

http://www.horrifictales.co.uk
Copyright © 2020 Stuart R Brogan

A CIP catalogue record for this book is available from the British Library

ISBN: 978-1-910283-29-5

ACKNOWLEDGEMENTS

Thanks to...

Graeme Reynolds at Horrific Tales for biting the bullet, Linda Nagle for hitting me with the editorial stick and Ben Baldwin for the outstanding art. Thanks to Jake Rose, Pete Rowland, Nev Murrey, Cat Dahman, Becky Narron, Mark Cassell, Kirsten Cross, Dean Samed, Matt Seff Barnes, Liz Williams and all the other authors/presses/ artists plying their trade within the publishing industry. Indirect thanks to John Carpenter, Neil Marshall, James Cameron, John McTiernan, Shaun Hutson, Brian Lumley, the country of Iceland, strong coffee, Orange Amplification, Jackson Guitars, Mossberg shotguns, harsh black metal, Cryo chamber and Hoyt Archery for stress relief, and of course my family and long -suffering wife, whose support means everything to me.

Last but by no means least, my readers, without whom my efforts would be lost upon icy winds - Thank you and I hope you enjoy this latest of adventures. If it's your first time aboard the Brogan crazy train, I suggest you buckle up, because things are about to kick off...

WILD HUNTERS

BY

STUART R BROGAN

CHAPTER ONE

Somerset, England – 876 AD

The blood-soaked band of battle-weary warriors gathered silently around the freshly-dug grave, the atmosphere malignant and foreboding, their flaming torches struggling against the punishing wind and relentless downpour. Most had not moved since claiming victory, the earth beneath them sodden, the bodies of their fallen brothers scattered all around.

The small clearing was silent but for the subdued chorus of heavy breathing and the constant drumming of rain upon steel. Above their heads, torn battle banners flapped in the wind, the otherworldly sound strangely hypnotic amidst the unimaginable carnage. For what seemed like an age, none dared speak, their thick tunics and heavy cloaks waterlogged, caked in the aftermath of the night's endeavours. With an air of unease, they kept silent watch over the tightly-bound corpse being lowered into the gaping void before them, the final resting place of the unnatural horror that had cost them so dearly that night.

Eventually, the tallest among them took a tentative step forward, the flame from his stave crackling and snapping with his sudden movement as if it, too, were desperate to flee this vile and cursed place. There came a muted gasp from more than one of the attendees. Still, the tall man edged ever closer to the precipice, grasping the hilt of his sword, ready to put steel to flesh once again should the need arise.

Above them, amidst the swirling darkness, an explosive clap of thunder preceded a flash of lightning which illuminated the clearing. In its glare, each man's face conveyed a frozen portrait of terror. Some of the figures huddled together, turning to the sky, each man convinced they had displeased their gods, fearful of swift retribution. Another loud detonation from above made three of their number lose their nerve and they began to flee. The tall man quickly turned and desperately tried to instil calm amongst his kin, but it was of little use. He helplessly watched on as yet more of his brothers ran for their lives into the surrounding forest, their forms instantly swallowed by thickets and ancient hollows. Those still devoted and loyal gave shallow nods to their leader, their splintered spears trustworthy and dependable, their iron-forged courage unwavering. The tall man gave the briefest of smiles and returned the gesture, silently acknowledging their sworn oaths and personal honour.

Only the bravest of men could undertake such an important and dangerous task and live to proclaim victory in the inevitable saga. This was no undertaking for those of spineless character, nor those who did not believe in the power of the old ways.

The Gothi ran a dirt-encrusted hand through his thick, plaited beard and eyed each of his men in turn, his stare penetrating the darkest depths of their very being. They silently looked on as he moved among them, fluid, yet cautious, as if studying helpless prey. When he was at last satisfied of their resolve, he stood before them once again and, in one swift movement, drew his sword and thrust it into the air, letting out a mighty roar. Those remaining followed suit, eager to join the primal cacophony and, as the storm raged around them, they raised axes, spears and swords in salute.

As one, they whooped and hollered, their ecstasy spurred on by the mushrooms and alcohol they had consumed by way of reward from their revered holy man.

The Gothi began to chant, quietly at first then with greater urgency, his abrasive tongue cutting swathes through the screams of rage encircling him. His words grew louder, his body a willing receptacle for the ancient powers of those who had come before him. Then, as quickly as it had started, all fell quiet as the men lay down their weapons and began to scrape mud and damp earth into the hole with their bare hands, their nails raking against rock and stone. Yet they did not pause, oblivious to injury or fatigue.

The Gothi looked on studiously as his men went about their work, and began to feel the welcoming sensation of relief. The binding ritual had been a success; he could feel the shift in energy around them, in the rocks, the trees, and the earth beneath their feet. With blood, steel and courage, the unnameable horror had finally been defeated, its remains discarded far from his own shores and those he held dear. He could at last breathe deeply, embrace the cold winter air, and raise the briefest of spirits.

Despite his love towards his own kind, he cared little for this new world and its Christ-worshipping people, nor for the plight that he and his men had so ferociously battled then secretly buried among them. It was not his concern any longer; his part in the prophecy had been fulfilled. Only the gods and goddesses could pass judgement over his actions, not man. Never man.

Before the last of the grave was filled, the Gothi reached under his filthy robes and retrieved a bundle of rags. With trembling hands, he began to unravel them. The bedraggled warriors watched in awe, edging closer for a better view as the tall man tugged a small spearhead free from its protective coverings and held it close to his lips. He closed his eyes and began to whisper the Galdr, the spoken rune magic of their ancestors. They remained silent, none wanting to break the holy man's concentration for fear of negating the spell's power or releasing the terror for a second time.

Once again, the Gothi glared at those gathered before him, daring each of them in turn to challenge his power.

None did, and with lightning speed, he threw the spearhead into the grave. No sooner had he done so than his followers fell to their knees once more and quickly set back to work. As the last remnants of wet earth were patted down, he felt satisfied. The area looked to be untouched once more. *Only the gods should know of this place.*

With brows damp and muscles sore, the men rested. The Gothi took time to silently acknowledge those who had partaken in the ritual. As another deafening crack of thunder ravaged the turbulent sky, they reached up in reverence to the storm and began to chant as one.

"Hail Odin, Allfather!

CHAPTER TWO

Somerset, England – Present Day

In little under five seconds, Sergeant Shaun "Smudger" Harper pumped the thirty-round magazine into the target. He heard the sharp metallic click as the bolt slammed back into the open position, and grinned. Faint wafts of gunpowder caught his nostrils as he tipped the rifle to one side. He detached the mag and worked the charging handle, his actions ingrained, automatic. He double-checked the breech, and once satisfied the weapon was clear, depressed the bolt. There was nothing better than getting some personal time on the range to blow away the cobwebs of inactivity.

Smudger slung the SA80 A2 over his shoulder and dug into his pocket to retrieve his small pack of tobacco. Once rolled, he cupped his hand against the wind, and lit the cigarette. He coughed as he inhaled the smoke, then gently let it go, the hit adding to his momentary euphoria. He took in the wintry beauty of his desolate surroundings; the range was now eerily quiet but for the wind and the increasing moan of leafless trees. He looked towards the peppered wooden targets a mere seventy-five feet in front of him, then further, to the horizon, towards the man-made hill that acted as a safety backdrop. The last thing the local farmers needed were stray rounds raining down on their livestock, not to mention onto some lost hiker exploring the Somerset countryside. The paperwork would be a nightmare.

To his left lay ten acres of dense and ancient woodland with a vast expanse of grassland running parallel, on which stood two pairs of green military tents, acting as the HQ and billeting for the weekend's live-fire exercise, much to the disgruntlement of his men. To his right was a barely-maintained access road, and beyond that, swathes of scrub that gently rolled away into the fields. During the summer, they were full of crops, but now in mid-December, they resembled nothing more than a muddy and barren wasteland.

Regardless of its surrounding beauty, Ham Hill MOD range was truly antiquated, yet, in Smudger's eyes, still served its purpose. In truth, it was secretly one of his favourites, the rough and ready appearance adding to its hardcore appeal. He was somewhat gutted, though, that the brass were planning on closing it down after many a year's faithful service. It was lacking by modern standards, with only a handful of low-lying buildings that included an office, a small kitchen, a shower block, and an armoury, but that was just the way Smudger liked it. It seemed the military were selling off everything. A sign of the times.

The principal users of the range were soldiers from all arms of the military, but on rare occasions, the facilities were utilised by select civilian shooting clubs, all eager to test their mettle in outdoor conditions. Smudger couldn't help but scoff. Thousands of pounds worth of kit, yet no clue about how to use it. Where were they going to shoot now? Or would some corporation buy the place and charge them astronomical fees? Regardless of the outcome, it wasn't his problem. He really would miss the place though.

Smudger let out a soft chuckle and went to take another drag but suddenly recoiled and dropped his cigarette.

"Fuck!"

He grimaced and nursed his burnt fingertip as he ground the offending roll-up underfoot, hoping none of his subordinates had witnessed this clumsy, unmanly display. He sighed deeply, his bones and muscles aching in the harsh bite of the winter's chill. He reached up and gently massaged his right shoulder, allowing his eyes to close. The relief was short-lived.

"Sarge, what else needs to get loaded on transport back to barracks?"

Smudger regained his composure and turned to the fresh-faced Marine who had addressed him, impressed by, and slightly jealous of his youthful features and tenacious spirit. He eyed him up and down shaking his head in mock disappointment.

"Are you some sort of bloody numptie, or what, Collins? Do you reckon we should just leave all this fucking hardware laying around for Farmer Giles or one of those muppets from the general public to play with?"

Smudger gestured over his shoulder to the five neatly-stacked flight cases sat at the rear of a trio of Land Rovers. Each case contained SA80 A2 assault rifles, personal kit and supplies, as well as an L110A1 Squad Automatic Weapon. Not to mention a few grenades and one little surprise the lads weren't privy to.

"Better yet, should we just sling it on eBay? Or go one step further and hand it over to a bunch of machete-wielding terrorists? We may only be Reservists, lad, but we're still Royal Marines!"

The young Marine remained stiff and silent for fear of reprisals, embarrassed for having asked such a stupid question. Should he respond? All he could do was stare blankly at his superior and wait for a clue.

"Well?" the sergeant snapped, sensing his unease.

"Um, no, Sarge. I ... I mean, sorry, Sarge."

Smudger shook his head again, then, after a few seconds, he began to grin broadly. He didn't have the heart to grill him—or to keep a straight face, for that matter. After all, he had never seen any action, nor was he doing the job full-time. He was usually to be found working in some air-conditioned canteen, chatting up young students, one of whom had just given birth to their first child. To say the young lad was preoccupied was an understatement; he found the magnitude of fatherhood daunting. Of course Smudger was in no position to give sound advice, given his own, undisclosed predicament, nor impart pearls of wisdom. He figured he should just keep his mouth shut and give the young lad a pass.

He looked up at the swirling mass of dark clouds gathering above them, the raindrops growing ever-forceful. The forecast had warned some severe weather was coming in from the Atlantic; the south-west had been put on red flood alert, but how often did they get it right? Well, despite Smudger's doubts, a torrential downpour did now seem likely. He huffed, tugged back his camo jacket sleeve and checked his watch.

"Right then, Collins, it's 15:00hrs and the range gets locked down at 18:00hrs. So as long as we get on the road by 17:45, you useless bunch of tossers can have a few hours downtime."

Collins remained motionless, unsure if his sergeant was testing him. Smudger sighed.

"Well, go on then, sod off. And tell the lads to get some scoff and a brew down them."

The young Marine grinned and stood to attention, silently relieved he had avoided a dressing-down.

"Yes, Sarge, thank you, Sarge." He saluted, took a step back, then turned on his heels, eager to relay the good news to his fellow Marines.

"Oi! Just make sure everything is stowed away first," Smudger yelled, "and that includes these weapons, you muppet!" His subordinate double-timed away towards the makeshift camp.

"And don't forget those boxes of surplus ammo from the armoury; the brass would have a fucking meltdown if you idiots left it here, and I sure as hell won't take a bollocking for you."

Smudger sniggered as he watched the young lad disappear into the mess tent, then listened as the silence was broken by a hearty and resounding cheer.

He hurried across the field to the welcoming shelter of his own tent just as a crack of thunder signalled the arrival of what turned out to be a torrential downpour. He watched silently as the ground outside was reduced to a bog of saturating water and clawing mud.

"Fucking marvellous," he muttered. At least he could take solace in the fact that this time tomorrow, he'd be lounging around watching movies or reading a good book. The rest of the lads could keep their precious football matches on the big screen down the local. To Smudger, there was nothing more tedious. Now, boxing. That was a real sport, practised with honour and humility, thuggish in appearance, yet scientific by design. A true art form, not to mention one of his personal passions. The sooner he could get back to the gym, the better.

As his tent reverberated with the constant impact of the rain, the weary soldier unstrapped his rifle and rested it barrel-up against his camp bed. He let out a slight moan of discomfort as he began to shrug off his webbing, his right shoulder gnawing again and sore. With a huff, he tossed the load-carrying equipment to the floor, glad to be rid of the extra weight. The beginnings of a headache were stabbing at his eyes.

As he slumped down onto his bed, his mind wandered back to his younger days, back when he first joined HM Royal Marines. The pride he had felt as a fresh-faced recruit, standing tall on the parade ground, receiving the coveted green beret. Nineteen years old. It had been the crowning moment of his life, a prize above all others. It was just a shame his parents couldn't have seen it. It had been a whirlwind adventure and one hell of a ride, but of course, all good things must come to an end. He had done his time now, paid his dues, and was proud to bear the scars of his service. Now, at the ripe old age of thirty-two, he was glad to be slowing down. Not ready for the scrap heap yet, but close enough to smell it coming.

Of course, it hadn't all been plain sailing. He left full-time service when he turned twenty-seven—not by choice, but because his now ex-wife had been unable to handle the lack of social life and the constant relocation. He had begrudgingly agreed to her ultimatum and, unsurprisingly, they split soon after, not only making him regret his decision but generating a bitterness towards women. All women. It was then that he took control of his own destiny and joined the Royal Marine Reserves, his time now split between labouring on building sites for a few quid and keeping a bunch of weekend warriors on task. He was still able to serve his country, though. That was the only thing that truly mattered.

The sudden rumble of thunder snapped Smudger from his reminiscence. He sighed once again and sat up, his eyes throbbing from the ever-increasing headache. He moved to his bergen on the far side of the tent but as he was retrieving a pack of painkillers, a new arrival announced its presence.

"Um, sorry, Sarge, got the CO on comms, says he needs you ASAP."

Smudger quickly washed down the tablets, the acidic taste making him gag slightly. He cleared his throat.

"Right, thanks, Downs," he growled quietly, "I'll be right there."

Downs — not your typical Marine, given his officious appearance and boyish frame — nodded and turned to leave. Smudger raised his hand, stopping him in his tracks.

"Make sure all the kit is stowed away ASAP; I want all the weapons accounted for and loaded, then tell the lads to break down the tents. It's not like the brass to get hold of us like that. I've got a funny feeling we'll be leaving sooner than expected."

Downs saluted, acknowledging the order, and disappeared. Smudger straightened up and tugged down his camo jacket—after all, he had to show those whippersnappers how a real Marine dressed. He put on his beloved green beret and adjusted it. *Best go see what the powers that be want.*

The rain showed little sign of easing, and Smudger could feel the liquid permeate his fatigues, though it was mere feet to the comms tent. He entered the tent and was greeted by the concerned faces of Marines Downs and O'Hagan, both of whom sat silently on a bench, their backs to the makeshift table that supported the comms equipment. Smudger nodded to the pair and grabbed the receiver. He sucked in a deep breath. He hated talking to the brass; pompous bastards, the lot of them.

"Sergeant Harper here, sir," he stated with as much conviction as he could muster.

"Um, yes sir, that's correct...Do we know how many? No problem. I'm sure me and my lads can handle it...We can be on-site within half an hour depending on weather conditions...Yes, sir, I understand. No, sir, my boys won't have an issue with that."

Downs and O'Hagan sat motionless, eager to know what was being said. The stocky Irishman scratched his cropped hair.

"Whaddya ya reckon, Stevie? What's the craic? Do ya reckon all's well aloft the ivory tower?"

Steve Downs merely shrugged, amused as always by his abrasive friend.

"Hell if I know, Liam," Downs replied. "Whatever it is, I'm pretty sure we aren't going to like it."

"Really? I thought you were supposed to be some clever, educated fucker?"

"I may have gone to Uni, but that doesn't give me access to the inner workings of those in 'charge.' Just going to have to see how it plays out. But by the look on Sarge's face, I reckon we are in for a night of it."

"Ah, bollocks," said O'Hagan. "I reckon it's bad news, Stevie. I wanna get back home. I've got me a sweet young lady lined up, and she loves herself a Royal Marine bad boy of the Celtic persuasion, know what I mean?"

Both men laughed, but abruptly stopped as they noticed Smudger glaring at them. He carried on with his conversation.

"Absolutely, sir, one hundred per cent on board, not an issue, sir. We'll check in at 23:00 hrs. And you, sir."

Smudger handed the receiver back to Downs, his face carefully masking the nature of the call.

"O'Hagan."

The Irishman stood to attention. "Sir."

"Go get the lads in here double-time, we're on the clock."

O'Hagan didn't need to be told twice. It was only a matter of minutes before the Reserves had assembled.

***

"Right then, lads, just got new orders from brass, and I'm afraid you ain't gonna like it..."

There was a muted grumble.

"...It would seem this shitty weather has cut off this part of central Somerset; it's flooded the Levels for ten miles in each direction. This means that there are approximately seven or eight villages within our reach, containing anywhere up to two hundred civilians, unable to escape the rising waters. Our orders are to make our way down into Westward Hay and start evacuating before it gets any

18

worse. From there we'll fan out and assist wherever needed. Any questions?"

"Sir," announced Downs, "I know I speak for the rest of the lads when I ask—how come O'Hagan here is such a wanker? And will he ever find a woman who will put up with his bullshit?"

"And his mum doesn't count," offered Collins, stuffing the remnants of a sausage roll into his mouth.

"Right bunch of funny fuckers, ain't ya, saying nasty things about my Ma," blurted O'Hagan, flipping the middle finger.

"Ah, don't be like that, mate. It isn't Collins' fault Mrs O'Hagan raised a bell-end!" retorted the smiling Downs.

Smudger waved his hand amidst the hilarity.

"OK, OK. Well, to be honest, lads, that is a bloody good question. In fact, one I too have spent many an hour pondering. In truth, nobody, not even God almighty, has a clue why O'Hagan is such a wanker. And with regards to him finding a woman who will put up with him, I bloody well doubt it!"

The laughter settled down, while the Irishman turned a shade of scarlet.

"Are we getting paid overtime for this?" asked O'Hagan. "Maybe even a bonus?"

"I bloody doubt it" said Downs. "No bullets flying, no extra dosh."

"Bollocks!" O'Hagan replied. "Extra hours, no shag, and fuck-all cash. Bloody story of my life, that is. Somebody remind me why I do this job."

"Because yer shite at flipping burgers, mate!" said Collins. "And anyway, no other fuckers would put up with ya!"

"Right then," said Smudger. "Settle down, ladies, back to business. Anyone got any serious questions or concerns? Preferably ones which have nothing to do with O'Hagan or his mum."

"Aye, sir. Is there any chance of help from the local bobbies or the fire brigade, or are we on our own?"

The question had come from his number two, Lance Corporal William "Fergie" Ferguson, whose courage and loyalty were unwavering. At six-three, Fergie still had a physique most men would kill for—no doubt an asset when growing up on the unforgiving streets of Glasgow's west side. The Scotsman had served full-time, seen his share of action, and was most definitely a man you wanted on your team if the shit hit the fan. A true warrior, and one of the nicest blokes you could ever meet.

"Nope, sorry, fella, it appears we're on our own, as per usual. The chopper coppers and County Search and Rescue have tried to get their birds up, but the weather's getting worse every second. They reckon it's too dangerous to fly, and to be honest, I don't blame 'em. The fire brigade's only managed to get two engines from Glastonbury past the floods and have now apparently lost contact. How exactly you 'lose' two bloody great, bright red fire engines is a mystery to me, but hey-ho. They also reckon there's no chance of getting more into the area any time soon. The eggheads estimate the rising water levels are already at five feet and showing no signs of easing, so it's pretty much impassable to civilians unless they own a Yank monster truck. We, on the other hand, are on high ground, slap-bang in the middle of the shit-storm, and as such, stand a better chance of getting to those who are trapped. The local authorities and emergency services have attempted to put the word out, but all comms have been cut off. No electricity, mobile reception, or bloody carrier pigeon for that matter."

There was an awkward flutter of humour, but Smudger noticed one or two concerned looks pass between them. He grinned to show there was nothing to worry about.

"Yeah, yeah, I know, lads, it's a fucking ball-ache for sure, but orders are orders. It looks like we won't be going home anytime soon, so let's get our shit together and show these cider-drinking locals how the Royal Marines operate."

"Sir, are you sure we ain't getting overtime, or at least danger money? It's dark out there. I might drown," O'Hagan griped, only half-joking.

"Yeah, Sarge," added Collins. "O'Hagan here is a delicate little flower. He hasn't even brought his water wings."

"Aye, cannae swim for shite, that one," said Fergie.

"Fuck's sake, pack it in, the lot of ya," replied Smudger, kicking the Irishman in the leg. "Do you ever shut up moaning, O'Hagan? Just put yer big boy pants on, grab yer rubber ducky and suck it up." He turned then to address the whole squad. "And try not to make me look bad. Got that?"

The four of them stood to attention and saluted. Smudger chest filled with something like pride.

"Good lads. Right then, I want to be on the move in fifteen minutes. The sooner we get on with it, the sooner we can get back to the world."

The tent suddenly burst into life as the Marines began to go about their duties.

Fergie moved in closer so as to not be overheard.

"What's on yer mind, mate?" asked Smudger.

"No mobile reception? No comms? What the hell could be causing that? How'd they got hold of us, then?"

Smudger shrugged.

"I don't know, fella, maybe 'coz we're higher up. Sorry, mate, I just haven't got answers for you, I'm just passing Intel down the chain of command. I suppose we'll find out in about thirty minutes." He feigned a smile and patted his friend on the shoulder.

"What about the surplus ammo we were supposed to transport to base?" Fergie asked. "I don't think it's a good idea taking it with us, especially because it's a civilian EVAQ. Should we maybe just secure it here and come back for it later?"

Smudger rubbed his forehead, weighing up his options.

"Yeah, I see yer point, mate. I don't really want to leave it here, though. With the weather and the local coppers busy, anyone could pay a visit and walk off with it, and it could be days before anyone realised. In all honesty, it's safer with us. Tell you what, we'll have someone on watch at all times, to keep an eye on it. How's that?"

"Aye, fair enough. But I reckon we should split the load between the vehicles, that way we can store them in the lock boxes and it's not all in the same place. No point advertising what we're carrying. What d'ya reckon?"

Smudger nodded in agreement and raised a smile, eager to lighten the mood.

"Agreed. Fine. Come on, Fergie, this isn't Kandahar, it's a friggin' cakewalk rescue mission in sunny Somerset, so let's stop fucking about and get to it, eh?" Smudger sensed something else was bothering the Scotsman.

"Well? I've known you too long not to notice when yer dancing around something," said Smudger. "Speak freely, mate."

"Look," said Fergie, "even before we left barracks, I wanted to say, you know...I'm sorry for what's happening with you and your little girl. The games Karen's playing are bang out of order. God only knows what you are going through. And, before you say 'you haven't got kids' to me, it doesn't mean I don't feel yer pain. It works both ways, remember. I've known *you* for years; I can see it in your eyes. Just wanted you to know I've got yer back, as always."

"I know that, mate," said Smudger. "Thanks. Didn't feel like sharing, is all. My 'man pride' wouldn't let me. It's just fucking hard, you know, my Stacy being raised by another man. Him being called daddy and all that; it sticks in my fucking throat, is all."

"Ya cannae reason with Karen? Come to some kind of arrangement?"

"I've tried, but when it comes to me, she has a right stick up her ass. She doesn't even answer my calls or emails anymore, everything has to go through her bitch of a solicitor."

"You got yer own representation, right?"

"Yer fucking joking? Nah, mate, I can't afford it. I'd have to sell a fucking kidney just for an initial meeting. In fact, I would probably have to sell both just to get them to send a fucking email. Karen got the house and everything in it, and I don't have a pot to piss in."

"Look," said Fergie, "when we get back, come round to my gaff. We'll get some beers in, and have a takeaway, just you and me, like the old days. Let's put our heads together and come up with a game plan. What d'ya say?"

"Yeah, mate, you know what, that would be great. The way I'm feeling right now, I could quite happily eat a fucking bullet."

Fergie grabbed him by the arms and slammed him back against the table, his face filled with fury and something else.

"Don't you ever say shite like, do you hear? Not to me, not ever again. I'll not have that kind of talk. I've lost enough pals that way. Got it?"

Surprised by his friend's reaction, Smudger nodded.

"Yeah, I— Jesus. Sorry, man. I'm just all fucked up at the moment. Look, thanks for looking out for me, I truly mean that. You saved my arse back in the desert and now yer doing it again. Seriously, thank you. And don't worry, I ain't gonna blow my brains out." Smudger turned away. "Anyway, I'm a shit shot. I'd most likely miss." His mouth contorted into something approaching a grin.

Fergie nodded, satisfied his friend had received the message loud and clear.

The air filled with a sudden clap of thunder. Together, Fergie and Smudger peered out as the sky turned black, massive cloud formations beginning to swirl and twist above them. Smudger turned to face his comrade, his head back in the game.

"It would seem, as always, that God loves Her Majesty's Royal Marines," he shouted over the storm.

Aye, but the Devil still wants his due, thought Fergie.

CHAPTER THREE

With the sound of grinding metal, Barry Yates forced the digger into gear and slammed his foot on the accelerator. The colossal machine lunged forward, its exhaust pipe belching thick black plumes of smoke. Barry leaned forward, straining to see through the rain-battered windscreen.

"Fucking useless piece of shite!" he yelled, and he gave the machine more power, his patience all but gone. The engine roared once again, the cabin shuddering as the caterpillar tracks suddenly found traction on the peat soil and waterlogged divots carved into the ground beneath.

"Come on, ya dancer!"

He manoeuvred the digger up a slippery bank and grinned as the metal monster tipped forward at last. He kept his cool, knowing full well that any lapse of concentration could result in the digger tumbling down either side of the bank. Not a great way to end up when you were on your own.

Barry loved his job. Turning and extracting peat for the local farmers was not only lucrative but it allowed him to spend time on his own, far away from the distractions of modern living. His drinking buddies down the local pub would poked fun at the grumpy old bugger for his unwavering views about the state of the world in general, but more specifically the decline and destruction of his beloved Somerset. To his mind, the further he was from those 'Townie' types with their fancy cars and modern gadgets, the better.

Despite his enthusiasm for working the land, Barry's

pet-hate was lousy weather—and in all his years on the job, this was the worst storm he had witnessed. But, for the amount of money his new paymaster was offering, he would happily put up and shut up. If it got any worse, he might have to admit defeat.

The old man edged the unit slowly forward and tugged on the handbrake. He left the engine idling as he opened the cab door, the wind nearly taking it off its hinges. Barry huffed as he pulled himself out of the unit and studied the area before him, his exposed face taking the punishing brunt of the wind and rain. *Sod it*, he mused, *might as well give it a go.*

He climbed back in, slammed the door, and once again put it into gear, his old-school resolve galvanizing his actions. Once in position, Barry grabbed the digger controls, activated the arm, and began to carve out swathes of peat with the cast-iron bucket, its teeth making light work of the topsoil. Of course, the heavy rainfall helped, but for the most part, Barry liked to believe it was all down to the skill of the operator.

The old man glanced at the cab's digital clock—18:32. He would give it another half hour then call it a night. There was no point in taking stupid risks, especially in this weather. Besides, steak pie was on the menu tonight, followed by a couple of pints of scrumpy. There was no way he was going to miss that.

With an incredible, ear-piercing metallic screech, the digger began to shudder, and the stench of hydraulic fluid flooded the cab. Barry gagged on a large lungful of infected air and grabbed the levers, his hands trembling and sore from the vicious vibrations. He could hear the mechanisms screaming, metal twisting as if the colossal engine had snagged on something but was unwilling to give up the fight. From below his seat, he began to hear the gearbox engaging, and he felt a sick wave of fear as the cab started to fill with acrid smoke.

For the first time in years, Barry began to panic. He

reached for the ignition, quickly turning the key and tugging it free. As he did so, the machinery juddered violently then fell silent. The old man let out a staggered breath, relieved he'd avoided a fire. His body was still shaking from the ordeal, so Barry took a few seconds to regain his composure. He pressed his face against the cool windscreen and controlled his breathing. He grumbled, his mood diminishing even further as, once again, he flung open the door. He'd have to go see what had caused the snarl up. Shielding his eyes from the relentless rain. he lowered himself down and scanned the surrounding area, but he could see nothing through the impenetrable cloak of darkness. The heavy machine's spotlights were now all but useless.

"Bollocks," he muttered, making his way around the outstretched loading arm and bucket, its shadowy outline akin to some enormous insect appendage, his poor eyesight only adding to its sinister appearance. He reached out a trembling hand and felt his way along the cold metal until he reached the very end. As he moved closer, his mind raced with possibilities, but it was most likely that the teeth had snagged something beneath the surface. He doubted it would be a significant problem for a man of his experience and hoped he could sort the issue with minimum effort.

As he reached the end of the arm, he noticed an area directly below the bucket that appeared a lot darker than the surrounding environment. Edging closer, he saw it was a hole—much bigger than he'd expected: twelve, sixteen feet deep, maybe. He couldn't have dug that. Barry studied the anomaly, its banks steep, walls interlaced with thick black roots. With one hand gripping the metallic limb, he leaned closer, trying to comprehend the appearance of such a void, but as his eyes adjusted, he began to realize the aperture itself wasn't the strangest thing; there was something else, something...moving within its gloomy depths—and that something appeared to be crawling towards him.

"What the hell?" he mouthed as the shape began to rise,

its outline somehow recognisable and alien at the same time, its movements jarring and purposeful.

The old man stepped backwards, his body unwilling to obey his command to flee. He furiously wiped his eyes, his vision still blurred by the relentless downpour. He scanned about him, desperate to locate some avenue of escape, for some explanation for what was happening. Still, his silent cries were greeted only by the clawing darkness closing in around him. He took another step back and shot an urgent glance towards the relative safety of the cab, then back at the void, the horror climbing ever upward. He shook his head in denial and began to mumble the Lord's Prayer as a rotting, clawed hand emerged, fingertips digging into the waterlogged earth, its colour mottled and diseased. Wispy tendrils of flesh hung from the nightmarish appendage, revealing bone and sinew. Barry winced as his nostrils caught the smell of decay and he stifled a scream as another hand appeared from the depths. Like the first, it began to dig its fingernails into the earth, eager to escape its prison.

The old man gasped, clutching at his chest, but finally found the will to move. He turned on his heels and staggered back round towards the cab, desperate to find sanctuary. Close behind him, he began to hear strange archaic mumblings, discordant shrills from what he had to presume was hell itself, as the creature dragged itself from the hole and into the raging storm.

The fleeing man crashed into the side of his vehicle but, as he reached out to pull himself up onto the digger's tracks, something struck him from behind, and the force of the blow sent him sprawling. He let out a scream of pain as his skull collided with the wet metal, then felt his legs give way beneath him. Crumpled on the ground in the water, mud and filth, Barry drew a deep breath and tried to focus up at it through his tear-filled eyes.

It appeared to be a woman, her torso and limbs frail, elongated somehow. Her body was loosely covered in what must once have been a plain white dress, but was now little more than a torn, dirt-encrusted rag. Her face was gaunt with high cheekbones that appeared to be the same colour as her ungodly fingers. Step-by-step, she edged closer, her movements awkward and unbalanced. Her form seemed to be changing, fluctuating from solid to semi-transparent. It like a half-tuned television channel, the static obscuring, then changing, allowing for a clearer picture. Barry began to whimper and gag as the stench of decomposition lay siege to his senses. With her soulless green eyes, the fiend studied him, her head moving slowly from side-to-side as if deciding what she might do with her newfound plaything. Barry kept quiet, his geriatric body and bones aching from the attack. She raised her right hand and extended a savage-looking finger then, slowly, she pressed her nail into his left cheek. The old man whimpered in terror and pain as the creature pushed deeper, then slowly dragged her nail downwards towards his chin, letting loose a torrent of blood that splattered both victim and torturer. As Barry screamed, the creature smiled and began to whisper once more in her ancient, abrasive tongue. Confiding in him, perhaps. Teasing him.

As abruptly as she'd attacked, the abomination retracted her claw and retreated, then she stood motionless, her arms outstretched. She gazed up to the heavens, and to Barry's horror, began to fill the night air with her throaty chant, indecipherable and inexorable. She flung her incantations like weapons and the the storm responded. The old man's broken body convulsed in agony as a deafening clap of thunder reverberated overhead, shaking the earth violently beneath him. With disbelieving eyes, he looked up into the storm to see a vortex of blackened clouds open above him. But as savage as the rain was, other things started to appear amongst the clouds: dark foreboding shapes descending towards him. He tried to look away but the spiral of insanity was engulfing him. It was hypnotic. He lay in silence as more and more creatures emerged from the darkness.

Before his eyes, hulking masses of grotesque beings

dragged themselves from the shadows of the earth, tiny elf-like creatures materialized from the air, their eyes alight with mischief and mayhem. And, as Barry looked on, they joined hands and began to dance merrily to some infernal music, inaudible to him. To his right, squat-looking creatures with tangled beards stood motionless, their dead eyes studying him, their heavily-built arms resting on rusted and brutal-looking axes. And amongst it all, the the woman's throaty cackles and shrills grew louder, reaching new crescendos as vivid green apparitions began to swirl and contort around her. Then, without warning, they collided together to form a pillar of twisting green light that burst into the night sky, causing the clouds above to erupt in a sudden flash that was equal parts beautiful and terrifying.

Barry was helplessly enthralled, sanity all but lost to this strange gathering of entities. His gaze hopped from one fanciful creature to the next, drinking in details of horror and madness. Then he noticed the humanoid shape moving swiftly towards him through the riot. Curiously, at that moment, he was no longer afraid. As the long-dead Viking warrior bore down upon him, swinging its sword, Barry Yates closed his eyes for the last time. And he felt glad.

CHAPTER FOUR

"What the fucking hell was that?"O'Hagan glanced over at his friend, the wind biting at their exposed and ever-reddening faces.

He shrugged. Truth be told, he didn't much care, but he felt somewhat obliged to calm Collins' nerves. By his reckoning, the bright green flash had originated a couple of clicks west of their current position. He couldn't explain what caused it, but he was pretty sure it wasn't an explosion. For starters, there hadn't been a bang.

"I dunno. Some local's transformer going pop, maybe?"

Collins shook his head.

"Plenty of water around at the moment to fuck with the power supply," O'Hagan added.

"I ain't no electrician, but what sort of bloody transformer explodes with green light, you Irish prat? The electric's all out, anyway, so how the hell's it supposed to explode?"

O'Hagan chuckled softly, amused by his mate's dramatic tendencies.

"Well, I dunno. Maybe it was some gas line igniting and the bloody weather stopped us hearing the bang. How should I know? And by the way, 'Irish prat' could be construed as a racial slur. I might have to bring that up with the Sarge, when we next have a little chat. I am sure you are aware, that could lead to disciplinary procedures, possibly even jail time. It'd be a terrible thing if a pretty boy like you became the bitch of the wing. My advice to you would be to wind yer neck in, maybe."

Collins smiled. He appreciated the distraction, though he still had some reservations about that flash. He playfully punched his friend on the arm and winked.

"Now you're just taking the piss, Mr Comedian. Right, come on, let's finish sweeping these houses. I'm cold, I'm hungry, and I want to get this over with."

They laughed nervously, slapped each other's shoulders, and began to wade through the waist-high water towards the semi-detached cottage. The weather was worsening if anything, but both men slogged on through the deluge.

At the perimeter of the dwelling, they paused and silently scrutinized the structure, searching for any sign of occupancy. There were no lights on. Neither of them spotted any movement nor heard any cries for help. If anyone was in there, they were probably tucked up cosy-like. Collins cupped his hands to his mouth and raucously announced their presence.

"Ello in there! Royal Marines here, we're here to assist you..." he yelled. Then, winking at O'Hagan, he continued.

"...Mr Farmer, please don't shoot us with your shotgun. My mate here is indeed Irish but he ain't here to rob ya!"

O'Hagan chuckled and thumped his arm, but he half-expected to hear the deafening reply of a twelve-gauge any second. He was relieved when none was forthcoming.

Apart from his mate's humorous—if somewhat overzealous—outburst, everything remained silent, the building itself shrouded in darkness. In the daylight and under better conditions, it would no doubt seem the quintessential English country farmhouse. The kind you see on those property TV shows, where rich people sell up and move on to their next dream abode. In the thunderstorm it looked positively ominous. O'Hagan figured anywhere would be better than here right now, especially since it was flooding.

As they drew nearer, Collins threw a glance over his left

shoulder, his curiosity still piqued by that mysterious green blast. The sky was black once more; the spectral anomaly had seemingly vanished as quickly as it had appeared.

"So, then, how does it feel to be a daddy?" asked O'Hagan. The question snapped the younger Marine from his musings. "Looking forward to shitty nappies and sleepless nights? You do realise yer life is pretty much over now, don't ya?"

"Mate, that is so fucking clichéd it's untrue," said Collins. "But to be honest, I'm bricking it. Lara's over the moon of course, and her mum can't stay away. Keeps popping by with shopping and clothes. Any excuse to visit. I can't get rid of the old dragon!"

"Yeah, I'd be scared shitless too, fella. She'll be after ya to quit this next and get yerself a shitty warehouse job."

"Yer just jealous," Collins spat, shaking his head.

"Well, I'll tell ya one thing, that ain't for me, mate. Ya can keep all that 'happy family' bollocks. I'm a man of action,me."

"Man of action? The only action you get is when you pay for it down the 'massage' parlour on the High Street. My Lara's classy, a real catch. I know Harrison wasn't planned, but I wouldn't change a thing, Liam. Not a thing. He's my world. If it means growing a set of balls and packing in the soldiering, then so be it. We all gotta man up sooner or later."

"Well, it's not my bag, but fair play to ya. Yer more of a dad than my old man ever was. Useless piece of shite, that man." O'Hagan felt a sudden surge of raw emotion, clutching at his throat. Something he hadn't felt since he was a child. He shook the thoughts from his mind.

"Lara's got a sister, doesn't she?" he added hopefully.

"Don't even fucking think about it!" snapped Collins. "I've got a gun, remember. Also, her dad's a raging headcase, and part of a biker gang. Done a stretch inside after pasting the last bloke who messed with his girls. Fucked him up good and proper. He likes me, though."

"Alright, I'll believe ya. What's her name? You know, the sister."

"Seriously, mate. Drop it. You got more chance of farting on the moon than getting off with Cassey."

"Ah, Cassey, is it? Cassey O'Hagan. It's got a nice ring to it."

"Fuck off, ya twat!" Collins huffed to O'Hagan glee.

"Ok, Mr Tetchy, calm yer horses. I'm just playing with ya. Right. Come on then, let's get it over with, and get back to the rest of the lads. I could murder a brew."

Together, they waded their way up the pathway towards the main entrance. They came to a stop when they saw that the front door had been left wide open. Overcome with a sudden wave of trepidation, Collins grabbed his flashlight from his pocket, thumbed the switch on, and directed the beam at the opening. It barely penetrated the gloom. The Marines hesitated, each man's mind urgently whispering of some unseen danger skulking in the shadows, yet elsewhere in the deeper recesses of their subconscious, another voice, soothing, bade them welcome. Commanded them. Without uttering a single word, both men advanced. Neither dared mention these powerful feelings, for fear of ridicule. Staying close together, they edged forward, stepped over the threshold, and entered the seemingly deserted house.

Neither man spotted the yellow eyes, glinting in the upstairs windows. Four sets. Watching them.

CHAPTER FIVE

Smudger sat silently studying the Ordnance Survey map, the page illuminated by a small Mag-Tec torch gripped tightly between his teeth. Other than the torch, the interior of the Land Rover was dark, its flimsy metal body rattling with the impact of the rain. Fergie took a final drag on his cigarette and tossed the butt out of the passenger window. He coughed and turned to face his friend.

"The water is nearly up to the top of the bloody wheels now; we're gonna need a friggin' inflatable if you don't make a decision soon."

The sergeant stayed silent, his expert eyes absorbing the map's details. Fergie drummed his fingers on the dashboard, eager to get started.

"Well? Where are we hitting next? Doesn't seem to be anyone around here. I reckon they got out before the main storm surge hit 'em."

Smudger took the torch out of his mouth and pointed it an area on the map.

"You bitch like a little girl, you know that?"

The Scotsman chuckled.

"Aye, I'm training to be an Englishman," he replied quickly. Smudger smiled at his friend's speedy quip.

"You ain't handsome enough to be English, mate," he fired back, and both men let out a hearty laugh.

"I reckon you could be right, though. It does seem everyone got out of Dodge. So—"

He adjusted the map as Fergie leaned in to get a better

look.

"—This is our current position. I think we should make our way up this road here, towards the village."

Smudger traced the route with his finger, pausing at what appeared to be a small hamlet approximately two miles due west.

"We got any Intel regarding the accessibility of this place? It looks like it's flanked on two sides by waterways, and peat moors on the other two. Pretty messy terrain. If the roads are gone, we might get ourselves stranded. Sure you want to take the chance?"

Smudger shrugged.

"We haven't been able to make contact with anyone since we left the range. I'm just winging it, mate; following my nose and seeing how things develop. Chances are, we're going to be stuck out here all night anyway, so we might as well have a scout about and do some loose recon. Don't seem to be many houses in this place, so it should be pretty straightforward to sweep. If it's empty, we can let the lads settle in for an hour or so to get a brew down them, maybe have a little kip. What d'ya reckon?"

Fergie stretched his arms and yawned.

"Aye, sounds like a plan. I'll get the boys together. We can finish off the last couple of houses here, then make our way up to the next RV. Providing the roads aren't any worse than this one, we should be able to ge—"

A commotion in the distance caused both men to pause and stare out of the windscreen, scanning the immediate area. Smudger shot Fergie a concerned glance, and as one, both men exited the vehicle, the Mag-Tec focused directly to the front of their position. Through the rain-battered darkness, Smudger made out a figure attempting to run towards them, but the deepening water hampered their progress. Fergie was the first to edge closer, as realisation hit.

"That's O'Hagan, what the fuck is he playing at? If he's messing around..."

Screams of terror rang out from the figure as he gained ground, interspersed with a string of incomprehensible words. At thirty feet, Smudger and Fergie were able to identify not just their Marine, but the words he was yelling. Four of them, repeated over and over again as he flung frantic glances over his shoulder.

"Get the fucking guns!"

Within seconds, the bloodied figure raced past them and barrelled his way to the rear of the Land Rover. He muttered to himself as he worked, his words disjointed, his breathing laboured, tugging one of the equipment cases free. For a matter of seconds, both men stood frozen. Nothing seemed to be chasing their man. Smudger was the first to react; he sprinted over to the Irishman just in time to see him slam home a thirty-round magazine.

"Whoa! What the fuck are you doing, Marine? That weapon is hot!"

The Irishman brought the weapon to bear and jammed the butt into his shoulder, his finger hovering over the trigger guard.

"You don't understand, sir! They came out of the shadows and got Collins, ripped him to fucking shreds! I barely got out of the house. They're fucking coming for us now."

He used the barrel of the rifle to point down the street in the direction from which he had come, shaking violently from the plunging temperature and bludgeoning fear. Smudger and Fergie turned to face the advance, briefly outlined by a distant flash of lightning.

There appeared to be a blackened crowd making their way towards them, their ranks two or three deep across the road. Fergie took a tentative step forward and squinted at the shadowy figures, their disjointed bodies and erratic movements casting ripples in the murky floodwater. He swallowed hard, shaking with the all-too-familiar adrenaline dump of engagement.

Smudger edged forward, scanning the skirmish line, desperate to assess the threat bearing down upon them. Suddenly, from their right, the familiar voice of Marine Downs broke the silence.

"Eh, Sarge, what's all the ruckus out here? I've searched the outbuildings and—"

Steve Downs stopped at the sight of his fellow Marines staring intently down the road, sullen and quite visibly shaken. He turned to face the same way and bringing his torch to bear, and for once in his life was lost for words.

Without hesitation, O'Hagan moved forward, letting out the cry to prompt immediate action.

"Contact front!"

Knowing full well what was about to happen, Smudger dropped down and turned away just as the Irishman squeezed the trigger. With an ear-splitting crack and a blinding muzzle flash, O'Hagan unloaded four quick semi-auto bursts towards the incoming atrocities. He laughed out loud as his rounds found their mark and tore into the first line of bodies, the impact sending dislodged bits of torso tumbling into the flood beneath them. Yet still they advanced, despite the sustained fire, their ranks replenished by countless other creatures crawling unabated from the darkness either side. On they came, an assortment of shapes an sizes, some gigantic, others more wiry and sleek. Skulking, cat-like shadows merged in and out of the shadowy landscape. O'Hagan turned to Smudger, his face contorting in terror and rage.

"They ain't going down!" he screamed, letting loose another couple of bursts. "They ain't going down! What the fuck?"

As soon as the second round of gunfire began, Fergie,

Downs and Smudger burst into action and took advantage of the Irishman's blistering attack. Keeping their bodies low, they sprinted to the rear of the vehicle, grabbing their rifles and gear. No words were exchanged as they slammed magazines into their weapons, tucking more into their webbing. The night around them was alive with the snap of machine gunfire. They raced forward, and in less than ten seconds, had set up defensive positions using the Land Rover doors, their kill zone clearly defined. O'Hagan let loose once again, hollering as the rounds blasted into his target.

All four looked on in disbelief as giant figures began to rise from the water: towering monstrosities devoid of facial features, their limbs strangely elongated, almost whip-like. Ever more apparitions appeared, not just from the burgeoning darkness nor even the flood waters, but from the air itself. Wispy, spirals of green began to morph and pulse above the attackers' heads, each one belching forth yet more hellish monsters eager to join the horde.

"What the fuck is going on? What's the order?" barked Downs, his limbs shaking.

Fergie scrunched his eyes tight, desperate to escape the mob bearing down on them, the madness of it all too much to take in. How could you fight *this*? It was Smudger's sudden and forceful command to "Open fire!" that finally dislodged his uncertainty.

All four Marines opened up, the intense strobing of muzzle flashes casting fleeting shadows across man, beast, and machinery. O'Hagan screamed in rage. The air resonated with gunfire and the hissing of hot casings splashing in the flooded road around them.

As the wall of horrors edged ever closer, Smudger began to make out some definitive features, finally visible in the Land Rover headlights.

The Royal Marine had never subscribed to the supernatural, nor did he put much stock in those who claimed to have had paranormal experiences. Still, as he stood his ground and reloaded, only one word came to mind to describe what he was seeing. They were trolls. Not the cute ones with bright pink hair you find in souvenir shops, but colossal beasts with monstrous limbs and repugnant, battle-scarred features. He glanced to the left as a number of tall, lumbering creatures, the likes of which Smudger had never dared envisage, dragged through the bracken-infested floodwaters, the ground shaking as they drew nearer. Flanking the main attack, Smudger spotted a small group of squat, humanoids, all-but obscured by passing shadows and the constant lashing of rain. The glimpses he caught were of dirty clumps of matted hair, arms and necks inhumanly thick. Despite their fearsome appearance, it was what they cradled in their grip or dragged behind them that unnerved him the most: a vicious battle-axe, blades pitted and burred with use and age. He froze momentarily as a trio of these monstrosities spotted him, and began to make their way towards him, breaking into a run. He called out a warning to his men and, as one, they turned to follow his finger. One of the creatures was now swinging something over its head and, still at some distance, it flung it towards them. The men watched in terror as six decapitated heads, lashed together with rope, landed with a splash in front of them. The faces were bloodied, eyes frozen in a look of everlasting agony.

With a hellish roar, the nearest dwarf was upon them, eager to put rusted metal to the flesh of its foes. Still reeling from the sight of the severed heads, Smudger managed to sidestep and the monstrous axe blade sailed just inches in front of his face, embedding itself in the door frame of the Land Rover. The vehicle rocked with the impact. Smudger regained his footing, his arms slamming the muzzle of his weapon into the creature's temple. He squeezed the trigger. With a blistering crack, he emptied his magazine into its skull. He smiled grimly as its head evaporated, leaving little more than a stagnant green mist. Smudger wiped the residue from his face and turned, sensing another attack. He braced himself but before he could raise his weapon, he felt the heavy handle of an axe connect with his temple.

With a sickening thud, Smudger was knocked from his feet and sent careering into the floodwater, his head ringing from the impact. Instinctively, he pulled his head back, desperate to keep his face out of the brackish water. He tried to stand, but his legs wouldn't respond. Chaos ruled. Through stinging eyes, he glanced up to see another kind of monstrosity swinging its weapon wildly down at him. The Royal Marine scrambled backwards, desperate to get out of striking distance, but the creature took a step forward. Then, abruptly, its head exploded. Its body wobbled for a moment, then fell uselessly to the floor mere feet from the soaking soldier. Fergie stepped forward, slammed his boot onto the decapitated monster's neck, and fired another ten rounds into its back for good measure. Fergie yanked the sergeant to his feet.

"Come on up, pal. There's work to do yet. Smudger retrieved his rifle and shook his head. The blow he'd taken left him nauseous. Around them, the sound of suppression fire still reverberated.

"Thought I was about to get my ticket punched there!"

"There's still time, mate, still time," Fergie replied.

Through this, O'Hagan and Downs had continued sticking it to the enemy. the floor around them awash with water and some other substance, slick on the surface.

Only four of the squat creatures remained and they began to retreat now into the safety of the storm. Smudger huffed forcefully, swung his weapon on target, and let loose a semi-auto burst.

"Fuck you, you cunts!" he rasped and one of the creatures dropped, its body disappearing beneath the waterline. A parting gesture, a message that he and his boys wouldn't go down without a fight.

Smudger held up a triumphant fist and waved it at the

horde. Futile but defiant. And the marines held their breaths. Strangely, the creatures stopped their advance, though their eyes were still fixed firmly on their prey.

The normally reserved Downs swallowed hard. None of them could take their eyes from the creatures; it felt as though to do so would break this fragile truce. He spoke to his CO from the side of his mouth.

"Sarge, what the fuck are those things? Where's Collins? What are they waiting for? We've done pretty much no damage to them; why don't they just finish us off?"

"I don't fucking know!" Smudger snapped, "but now's not the time to get sloppy, lads. Keep yer sights on 'em. Take turns reloading. If they move another inch, let 'em have it."

The three men nodded and obliged, their knuckles white as they held their foregrips, struggling to keep on target.

"This is some messed up shit!" moaned Downs. "Let's just get the fuck out of here, eh? Call it a draw."

"Shut it!" hissed Fergie. "Keep it together."

Smudger levelled his breathing and studied the creatures before him. He wiped the last of the ichor from his eyes, and tried to think of a way out of this. The heaving throng of horrors seemed to move restlessly, though it did not advance.

"Stand by," warned the sergeant. "Wait for my command."

It seemed as if the creatures were separating, allowing something to pass unhindered through their ranks. The bedraggled Marine looked on as the crowd split in two. Each group huddled together, heads lowered in apparent reverence for the lone figure which was making its way through the gap. At that distance, it was hard to tell what was approaching, but whatever it was, it looked a damn sight more human than the others. Judging by its reception, there was little doubt that this was their leader. It moved slowly yet purposefully towards the Marines, its progress fluid and unhindered by the floodwaters.

"What the hell do we do, sir?" Downs snapped as the figure gained ground. He stretched his index figure outside the trigger guard to ease the ache, then replaced it, ready to fire on command, his right eye glued to the sight on his rifle. The others followed suit, the tension tangible.

"Hold your fire, lads. I want to know what the hell caused them to back off, and this one might just tell us."

Fergie locked eyes with his friend and nodded silent agreement, knowing full well the ramifications of his actions if things went south.

The approaching figure appeared to be a woman, her frame slim and wiry, her body swathed in a dirty and sodden dress. She stopped ten feet in front of them, her ethereal features now fully illuminated by the Land Rover's headlights.

Smudger moved forward towards her, his gun steady. Fergie shot him an urgent glance.

"What the fuck are you doing, Shaun?"

Smudger raised his hand and waved it gently. The Lance Corporal understood: *stand by until instructed*, and he gripped his weapon.

The Marine took another step, while the female creature remained still, her green eyes unwavering.

Her features appeared smooth and feminine, her eyes a vivid emerald. Even at this distance, he could tell she was beautiful. His heart swelled as she smiled, warm as the sun.

"Why do you resist?" Her voice was eloquent and somehow sensual.

The Marine remained silent; his finger stayed poised on the trigger, the muzzle levelled at her torso.

"Why do you deny the Hunt?"

Smudger cleared his throat, but his voice still caught.

"What the hell are you? And what the hell are those things?" he croaked, gesturing towards the crowd of creatures. "What the fuck do you want?"

The woman cocked her head and held her hands up, almost as if in surrender.

"So many questions, my fearless warrior, the answers to which you couldn't comprehend. With regards to your more immediate dilemma, surely a man like you must realise that you stand no hope of survival, let alone victory. You must grasp the notion that instead, the ancient ones have called you to join us; your fates have already been decided by powers you cannot even begin to fathom."

She extended a hand towards the Marines, palm open.

"Lay down your arms, and we shall embrace you, not as enemies, but as kin."

And he did see it: the hopelessness of their situation, the inevitability of their deaths. Who, after all, could think to face a horde like this and escape? And something inside of him bared its teeth. Smudger sniggered, his body shaking, caught between fear and a well-rehearsed sense of 'fuck you." He cleared his throat and kept his voice even.

"I reckon I'll be the judge of that, Miss. Now tell your freakshow to back off, or things are going to get messy."

"Sarge, just shoot the fucking bitch!" barked Downs.

"Just say the word, boss!" yelled O'Hagan.

It was the woman's turn to laugh, and as she did so, the mass of horrors drew in behind her. Smudger pulled the rifle tighter into his shoulder, preparing to fire.

"I will give you and your brethren one last chance to submit. Join the Hunt or be forever damned. What say you, warrior? Choose wisely."

"Miss, no one has ever accused me of being wise, so, we'll take our chances, if it's all the same to you."And with lightning speed, he dropped to one knee, below the line of fire.

"Light 'em up!" he roared.

Like a well-oiled machine, all four soldiers began to fire, their sights firmly set upon the woman in front of them. She screamed as a wave of rounds hit her body, each tearing a hole in her torso, sending geysers of blood in an arc around her. Behind, the horde began to howl in rage. As her body fell back into the torrent, Smudger held up a clenched fist and the chorus of gunfire ceased. He got to his feet and edged toward the downed and floating body, its flesh shredded by the tsunami of lead.

The Marine sergeant leaned closer and prodded the body with the muzzle of his rifle; it bobbed there, limbs outstretched and limp. One down, he thought, fully expecting it to be his last.

"So much for the fate of the ancient ones," he snipped. The water in front of him erupted skyward as the decomposing figure lunged towards him, her hands clamping tightly around his throat, nails embedding in his flesh. He tried to struggle free, but his attacker was too strong. He lashed out with his free hand, but the strike had little effect. He gasped and struggled to no avail. Whiteness filled his vision as his brain became starved of oxygen, his fingers opened and his weapon fell useless to the floor.

As the world began to fade, he found himself staring, not at the face of a beautiful woman, but a rotting and diseased creature, her eyes now black and misty. The reeking stench of death emanated from her pores, but he could barely take it in, so tight was her grip. She let out a throaty cackle and pulled his face closer.

"My turn," she hissed.

CHAPTER SIX

South-East England - Undisclosed Location

The room was brightly lit, the florescent bulbs glaring upon the metal table and sparse furnishings. An uneasy silence hung in the air, the four occupants giving pause to the somewhat one-sided conversation.

"Well then, gentlemen. Let's start again, shall we?" announced the stern man at the head of the table.

He eyed each of his subordinates with obvious disdain. He had never trusted so-called experts and, more than likely, never would.

"For the purposes of clarity, am I speaking English? How many ways do I need to phrase the question before answers are forthcoming? What do we know? And please – no assumptions, just the cold, hard facts."

The three white-coated lab technicians remained silent, their eyes fixed firmly to the floor, none wishing to anger the man any further.

"Gentlemen, I like to think myself a tolerant man. However, I'm beginning to lose my patience. In approximately one hour, I will be heading back to London. I have no time for game-playing, nor time-wasting. Now, tell me what information you have regarding the acquisitions, and make it snappy."

He jabbed a well-manicured finger towards the nearest man and read out his name tag.

"Doctor Bowton. You seem like a sensible fellow. I'm fairly certain we haven't met before, but you at least know of my reputation. Pray impart some good news; I trust you do actually have some viable information, considering the creatures have been in your possession for well over a month. You haven't been idle, surely? You and your fine fellows here are supposed to be the *crème de la crème*, after all."

Dr Phillip Bowton shuffled nervously in his seat, his eyes flitting to his colleagues. He ran his hand through his scruffy brown hair and regarded the well-dressed gentleman who held them in such a dangerous grip. He couldn't help but notice his eyes. Cold, emotionless, concealing a deep intelligence. He was correct in one matter: they were all, of course, aware of his reputation. None of them needed it proved first-hand.

"Um, well, we aren't entirely sure of their origins. Their bio-molecular and cellular structure is unlike anything we've encountered before. In truth, we know very little and we – all of us – are still running tests. We should know more in the coming weeks."

His inquisitor leaned forward, menacingly. "But...?"

Dr Bowton swallowed hard and cleared his throat.

"We know for certain that they are both females. Mother and offspring, most likely. They don't eat meat as far as we can tell, and have only consumed vegetable scraps, albeit begrudgingly. None of my staff have witnessed any aggressive tendencies. As for where they originated, we simply have no idea. Of course, we know they were apprehended in a Scottish glen, near to a village called Talisker. That's on... er..." one of the other experts leaned in and whispered. "Ah yes, thank you. That's on the western edge of the Isle of Skye. Apparently, they'd been visiting a remote farmstead where, I am told, the young daughter of the owners had been feeding, and subsequently, befriending them. None of the family members have mentioned anything out of the ordinary regarding the creatures' behaviour, nor have they shown any signs of, um, cross-contamination."

"A good start, but how exactly did they come to be in our possession?"

"From what I've been told, the father of said child is a devoted Christian and, true to religious form, believed that they were 'evil' in nature, sent by the devil himself. He then alerted the local authorities who, unsurprisingly, believed him to be stark raving mad. But, as luck would have it, one of the local officials is on our payroll and subsequently alerted our team in Edinburgh. They managed to not only suppress any public interest, but also capture and deliver them to us for further study."

The well-dressed man eased back in his chair, cold eyes scanning the experts gathered before him.

"I take it the family haven't made any waves regarding the whole affair? I'm sure you have heard how distasteful I find the tabloids and other such unwanted press?"

Bowton nodded enthusiastically; he had at least some vestige of good news to impart.

"You are correct, sir, they have been extremely compliant. The ten-year-old daughter, has naturally been vocal, but nothing we can't discredit should the need arise."

"And they in our custody?"

"Yes, sir. The father and daughter are in this very facility, held under the pretence of quarantine. The possibility of a viral or bacterial contagion cannot be easily dismissed. The mother remains at the family home and has shown no interest in our involvement since receiving payment for their, um, inconvenience."

The cold-eyed man seemed less happy with this final piece of news.

"Indeed? How lax. I suggest that all three of them find themselves in a tragic accident soon, then. A car veering into a remote loch seems appropriate, wouldn't you say?

Loose ends, Dr Bowton, another of my pet peeves. So, then, moving on. What are your thoughts regarding our non-human guests? You have said they're not aggressive. Are you then of the opinion then that they pose no threat? None at all?"

The nervous doctor looked to his peers for assistance, well aware of his drift. They remained silent, relieved to be out of the spotlight for now. He took a sip of water and replaced the glass on the table.

"Um, sir, at the risk of speaking out of turn, we just don't have enough data. It would be immoral of me to, er, condemn a sentient life form. That is not the purview of science, as I'm sure you understand."

"Just humour me, Doctor."

"I'm sorry, sir. I cannot. They could very well be harmless. And, based on what we have observed so far, I am starting to believe that is the case."

"How long have you worked for us, Doctor? More to the point, how long have you overseen your department?"

"Ten years, give or take."

"And, during your illustrious career, how many non-human lifeforms have you come into contact with? And, out of those, how many meant us harm? Don't be coy, take a guess."

"I would say ninety-eight percent. But that's not to say this particular one falls into that category. In my opinion, they are indeed innocuous, and I shall continue to say so until proven otherwise. I flatly refuse to condemn a hitherto unknown life form to death just because it suits your politics." Bowton was by no means a brave man but he could feel his anger swelling in the face of such reckless arrogance. To hell with this man!

"Sir, am I correct in assuming that you have already made up your mind? That you will be ignoring our findings?

If so, I'm sure the board will have something to say about your disregard for scientific rigour. In fact, I have every intention of informing them of what has transpired here today, and I'm sure my colleagues would agree. You have overstepped the mark, and I for one will not stand idly by —"

The single gunshot was deafening within the confines of the sterile room. Bowton's companions looked on in horror as his head rocked violently backwards, a gaping hole where his left eye had once been. His body and chair tumbled to the floor, splashing their lab coats with blood and brain matter.

Sir Malcolm Hawker got to his feet, secreted his pistol once more, and tugged at his crisp white shirt sleeves.

"What a pity. Such a waste of talent. I feel sorry for the person who has to clean that up."

He eyed the remaining doctors, who remained deathly silent and visibly shaken. The old man grinned.

"Now then. Who's up for a promotion?"

CHAPTER SEVEN

Johnathan Brewer was on the verge of losing his mind. He wiped his brow before reaching for the camper-van's ignition for the fourth time in as many minutes. He twisted the key. A click. A brief buzzing noise, then silence.

"Jesus fucking Christ!" he exclaimed, before paranoia forced him to abandon his attempts and stare out of the window once again. He thumped the steering wheel with a clenched fist.

The vehicle was useless, that was painfully obvious. It had been stationary for ten minutes. The floodwater was up to the wheel arches now, and, as far as he knew, in the exhaust system—too much for the van to take. The van had performed admirably, despite its age, and he considered himself lucky to cover the two miles before it had succumbed to the inevitable. But what to do now?

The idea of making his way on foot to the nearest town in this weather was simply foolhardy. Not to mention the small fact that the horror he had witnessed was prowling the shadows out there somewhere, her minions close at hand.

She had laid her own eyes upon him and most certainly knew the part he had played in her re-awakening. For the life of him, he could think of no reason why she hadn't killed him. He had been alone, unarmed and, not being a brave man, couldn't have put up much of a fight. The only logical answer was that she wished to toy with him, perhaps prolong his suffering. Needless to say, he had to find somewhere to lay low and hopefully avoid detection long enough for her to lose interest. He had a slim chance of succeeding, but to say his options were limited was an understatement. "Think, man!" he bellowed, willing a viable plan to present itself. It did not.

What's done is done, no point dwelling on past events. He could try to guess her reasoning until the end of days but never reach a conclusion. 'The end of days' – how fitting.

Despite the severity of his predicament, Brewer was aware that now was not the time for knee-jerk responses. He had to stop, think, then act decisively. After taking stock and weighing up his options, his plan of action became clear and he felt briefly pleased with himself. His safe haven was near enough to reach on foot and secure enough for him to remain undetected. Of course, the real danger was getting there unscathed.

He got to his feet and manoeuvred his way out of the driver's seat back into the campervan's living quarters. He pulled on a thick jumper, then took a few moments to prioritise.

He rummaged in the drawers, his mind racing about all the things he might need. He paused then, concluding that speed was more important, given the circumstances and the distance he had to cover. He had little in the way of food and supplies in the van anyway, and no weapons. Right now, it was best to deal with the more pressing concerns. Getting there.

A scream from the surrounding darkness broke his concentration.

He froze, instinctively and outside beyond the rattle of rain on his roof, he heard shuffling sounds, water breaking against the vehicle's chassis, muttered words interspersed with low grunting. He daren't move. Not an inch. The van's windows all had their blinds pulled down, much to Brewer's relief, and all windows locked. Whatever was out there would hopefully just pass him by.

The van rocked violently as something big made contact with the rear end. He whimpered softly as the unknown thing dragged along the outside of the vehicle. He had the absurd image of being passed in a corridor by a sumo wrestler. Brewer followed the sound as it pushed its way forward towards the cab, then tried not to scream when it abruptly stopped. There was another loud bang as the vehicle was struck again, this time from the front, with seemingly deliberate force. Again, Brewer remained silent, clamping his hand over his mouth as he lost his footing and collapsed onto his bed.

From this crouched position, he watched quietly as a dark shadow moved past the windscreen, its mass almost the width of the vehicle itself. Then he heard yet more sounds: a woman screaming, a throaty growl, and the sickening, unmistakable snapping of bone.

Brewer got to his feet and edged forward to get a better look as the creature moved trudged away from the vehicle, clutching something in its hand. He kept vigil, eyes straining through the pelting rain, but he could see no real defining characteristics beyond sheer size. Suffice to say, its body was muscular, its arms thick and long.

Once the creature was clear, Brewer slumped down into the passenger seat, cradling his head in his hands. It wasn't the beast itself that horrified him the most, nor the thought of it coming back with others of its kind. In those last few moments, the thing that caused his stomach to churn was the sight of the dead woman being dragged along by one leg, her torso ravaged, her head only attached by the thinnest of cord of muscle.

After a few minutes composing himself, he got to his feet and moved quickly. He reached beneath his bedding, retrieved a small bundle of rags and, once checked, stuffed it under his jumper. After a final look around, he exited the van. It was time to move. Now or never.

He had barely started to wade through the floodwaters when he noticed something bobbing towards him. He reached down and retrieved it, curiosity getting the better of him. It was a woman's purse, sodden and blood-spattered. The victim's. He opened it, thumbing through a small selection of notes and various credit cards. And there was a photo. He stared at the image: a young girl, eight to ten years old, smiling at the camera. Her arm was draped over a large German Shepherd. For a split second, he debated holding onto it. A record of those lost. In the end, he tossed it away. It really wasn't his problem. They would hardly be the only victims that night.

Willing the brief encounter from his mind, he pressed forward, getting ever more soaked, his direction of travel the same as the gigantic creature – an unfortunate, yet unavoidable turn of events.

He heard strange noises amidst the unrelenting howls of the storm. Some were akin to tortured screams. Others, more bestial barks. But there was something else, something unexpected, pulling at his consciousness. He dismissed such irrational thoughts and decided to concentrate on his place of refuge. He was tired, hungry, and under a tremendous amount of stress. Yet, as he tried to keep his priorities straight, he heard the sounds again, and this time there was no mistaking them.

It was the sound of distant gunfire.

CHAPTER EIGHT

In unison, the three remaining Marines, powerless to intervene, let out a gasp at the sight of their commanding officer so brutally cast aside. Shock immobilised their battered and aching limbs for what seemed like an age.

It was the Scotsman who was first to act, though his mind was a vortex of fear.

"Smudger!" he rasped through clenched teeth, tossing his weapon to Downs without a second thought. Fergie motored forward; he couldn't fire with his oppo so close to the intended target.

As he charged, he reached behind him and tugged free his combat knife. *A last-ditch effort to even the score.* O'Hagan let out a warning cry, the entourage of hate now coming at them for a secondary attack. Downs and the Irishman immediately rushed forward, weapons raised, fanning out either side of the Land Rover to cover their besieged brothers. Both men swallowed hard as they began to scan the darkness closing in around them, the environment squirming as it came alive and spewed forth even more atrocities from some unseen and remorseless other-world. In a matter of seconds, the cries of "Contact left!" and "Contact right!" echoed, swiftly followed by the familiar crackle of machine gunfire.

Fergie ignored the incoming threat and kept going, his limbs burning. As he bore down on his target, he raised his arm slammed the blade home with devastating power. The she-beast let out an ear-piercing shrill as the knife pierced the base of her skull and burst through her throat. Enraged, she tossed Smudger aside and he hit the water-logged tarmac, his face and chest taking the brunt of the collision. Fergie tried to keep his focus on the injured creature, struggling in his grip. To his relief, and from the corner of his eye, he saw Smudger stir. Still alive! Fergie snarled now, and began to twist the blade, his body screaming for oxygen as the thing reared backwards, thrashing wildly, trying to shake him loose. Palms saturated from the putrid ichor, now flowing freely, the Glaswegian found his grip beginning to loosen. Around him, the area was incandescent with the gunfire once more. Another sortie being repulsed, maybe. The creature finally managed to turn, jarring his arm something fierce. With a vicious back-hand, he was thrown to the floor. A voice came then, out of the dark, a single word that cut through the chaos like music to his ears, followed by a springy metallic click. Fergie sucked in a massive gulp of air, ducked beneath the water and closed his eyes. He could just picture the familiar oval shape arcing over him.

With a mighty boom, the grenade detonated, deafening at such a close range, sending a massive funnel of water ten feet into the air. He felt the shockwave travel around him, heard the sound amplified beneath the surface. Above him, the woman had just enough time to shriek as the explosion took her off her feet, fragments tearing through her flesh and soft tissues. Not that it would keep her down. Amidst the raging firefight, O'Hagan and Downs saw the concussion blast catapult their foe backwards twenty feet or more.

In a whirlwind of snarls and shrieks, the horde halted their advance once more. These weapons brought to bear against them were like nothing they had seen before. There was hesitation there. Uncertainty. How had their queen been so injured? Despite this sudden reversal of fortune, a handful did still seemed willing to press their attack. Downs and O'Hagan quickly reloaded, bellowing curses as they opened fire once more.

Fergie resurfaced from the murky deluge, his head ringing from the cannonade, face bloodied from the small but savage wounds on his forehead and cheeks.

"Fucking hell, mate, you scared the holy shite out of me!" Downs squealed, half-turning. "You OK?"

Fergie coughed hard, his lungs desperate to pump the filthy liquid from his airways. He gave the thumbs-up, as he finally gasped in the cold night air, his body racked with aches and wounds.

Downs brought him up to speed between bursts of gunfire. "We hit the bitch with a fragmentation grenade. Sent her back to hell, boss."

"That crazy Celt has got those things on the back foot, but I don't think we have..."

"...much time left before they have another pop at us."

"I reckon we should get the fuck out of Dodge."

Fergie took his weapon, which Downs had retrieved, and ejected the magazine. It all seemed fine. He checked the rounds then slammed it back in.

"In that case, let's grab Smudger and get the hell out of here."

The sky erupted with a savage clap of thunder, sending ripples across the water's surface. They looked up to see a fork of lightning, snaking and twisting, carve the blackness in two. Its ferocity was unearthly.

"Where the hell's the Sarge?" yelled Fergie, trying to be heard above the echoes of thunder. Downs could only shrug. In truth, he had lost sight of his CO as soon as the grenade had detonated, disorientated in the ensuing chaos.

"I dunno, mate. I think he's gone, but I don't know for sure."

Fergie looked about him, scanning the blackened water, desperate to locate his friend. There! A figure stumbling towards him, arched and slumped, its movements slow.

"Shaun!" he yelled. As the Scotsman reached him,

caught him up in a tremendous bear hug, he could see that his friend was smiling.

"Don't worry, Jock; you ain't getting rid of me that easy."

"Jesus, man," snapped Fergie, "stop fucking about, ya prick. I thought ya was a goner!"

A deep growl behind them snapped all them out of their elation. Fergie turned to see what horrors were nearly upon them.

"Fucking leg it!" he screamed. Nobody needed to be told twice and, injured or not, Smudger had no intention of dying at the hands of some nightmarish fairy-tale. As they pelted towards the three Land Rovers, Fergie paused. "O Hagan!" he bellowed. "We're moving. Get the fuck back here, double-time!"

Pausing now and then to lay down suppression fire, O'Hagan began to back away, still yelling his fearsome invective. Meanwhile, Fergie, Smudger, and Downs had reached the closest vehicle.

"Get it started!" Smudger yelled as Fergie ripped open the door and dove behind the wheel, frantically snatching at the ignition. Smudger tugged open the passenger door and rested his rifle barrel in the crease between the frame and the door, ready to lay down covering fire.

With a sudden biting whine, the Land Rover turned over, its engine roaring to life. Smudger smiled as the reassuring sound flooded his senses, sending a new-found sense of hope through his entire body.

"Everybody in!" he shouted, as O'Hagan arrived. The Irishman pulled open the rear door and dove headfirst into the vehicle, just as Fergie slammed the Land Rover into reverse. Smudger threw himself onto the passenger seat as Fergie spun the steering wheel, causing the front end to skid in a wide arc. The flabbergasted Marines faced the rear window as the horde fell upon them, their vehicle rocking violently with the impact of the first ten or so creatures. They held on, the Land Rover sliding to one side, struggling to maintain traction.

"What the fuck now? Don't these things ever give up?" barked Downs as a colossal hand ripped its way through the roof. The creature began to tear back the bodywork with an ear-piercing screech as if it were peeling an orange. Downs bellowed in fright as the troll's gnarled and contorted face peered in at him through the hole, its pupil wide.

"Suck on this, ya wanker!" O'Hagan snarled, and he thrust the barrel of his rifle up through the hole squeezing the trigger. With a roar, the creature tumbled backwards off the roof, its face riddled with bullet holes, it's eye a gaping cavity. Fergie managed to get the vehicle into first gear at last, and powered through the water, leaving a considerable wake. Behind them, the night echoed with screams of primal rage.

As they sped up, the Marines aimed out of the windows and opened fire. Fergie didn't dare look back; his attention was firmly set on the submerged road. He leaned forward, straining to see through the rain-swept windscreen and the impenetrable blackness that seemed somehow more than night. The Land Rover's headlights were practically useless in this deluge.

"C'mon on, boys, talk to me, what the fuck is going on back there?" he yelled.

O'Hagan answered first. "well, them bastards don't like the grenade we force-fed their mummy!"

"Aye, we didn't even get the chance to give her pudding!" Fergie fired back with a gruff laugh. Smudger had been keeping an eye on the horde in his wing mirror, and he was pleased to see the last of the horde had fallen from view at last, swallowed by darkness and distance. He turned to Fergie and punched his arm.

"Fucking top work, fella. Guess I owe ya big time, eh?"

Fergie grinned and winked at his mate.

"It's beginning to get a bit fucking old. I should get danger money."

Downs chirped in, his voice tinged with trepidation.

"Sorry to be the party pooper, but what the fuck is going on, Sarge? I mean, what in the name of fuck just happened back there? And what happened to Collins? Shouldn't we go back to find him?"

"He's gone," said O'Hagan, "Trust me. I saw it with my own eyes."

An uneasy silence fell upon the occupants, each man momentarily lost in their own recollections, trying to put it all together in a way that made sense. Dead. They were fucking Reserves, out for a weekend jolly. How could he be dead?

Smudger sighed, long and low. "He's gone, lads, and there ain't nothing O'Hagan could have done. We've all seen these things, how they move, how they fight. It wasn't his fault. I don't know what the fuck these things are, but we're lucky to still be alive." He turned to face Downs.

"Look, I ain't got any answers for ya. Could be something those eggheads at Porton Down have cooked up. Fuck knows. Maybe they've given us some trippy experimental drug, watching us to see what happens. Those fuckers'd have zero remorse. Probably laughing their arses off right now.". He waited to see if anyone was buying this bullshit. Undeterred, he continued.

"Think about it. It makes perfect sense. The EVAQ of civilians, the training exercise, the storm to cover their tracks if things go sideways. We just *happened* to be in the neighbourhood, did we? Like shit. Expendables, us. Tossed into the meat grinder, all in the name of science."

He studied each man in turn. Nobody said a word; their faces spoke for them.

"We all know what they are," said Downs, "but we're too afraid to admit it—"

Fergie wasn't.

"—Demons." He glanced across at Smudger. "They're demons, aren't they." It wasn't a question.

"Demons my arse!" O'Hagan blurted, "there ain't no such thing. Only nut-jobs believe in that stuff."

Fergie wiped his face, his eyes stinging from the relentless concentration.

"Well, lads, I don't give a fuck. They come at us again, they're gonna get more of the same. Demons or not, they're gonna wish they stayed clear. Bring the aggro...?"

"Get a kicking!" they replied in unison.

"Too fucking right," said Fergie. "OK, Smudger, what's the play? I hope you've got some sort of bloody master plan, big man because, much as I hate to state the obvious, we just got our asses kicked by a bunch of fairy-tale fuckers from hell. It's time to shine, brother."

Smudger let out a laboured breath and cleared his throat.

"Well, as far as I see it, our choices are limited until they can get the choppers out, and that ain't happening in this storm. So. I reckon we're gonna need to find a decent layup point, prep our gear, dig in deep and get ready for them..."

"You saying they ain't finished with us, Sarge? You reckon they're coming back?" Downs croaked.

"Fella, I ain't gonna lie, haven't got a clue. But rest assured, if they do come back, they're gonna regret it."

For the next five minutes, nobody said a word, each man studying the environment for a suitable site.

"What d'ya reckon, Fergie?" asked Smudger, tapping the

windscreen and pointing.

"Aye. That'll do nicely, old chum."

They surveyed the small, steep hill, and the small church nestled at the top. The structure itself was approximately fifty feet away, with a narrow gravel path winding its way through a small collection of gravestones towards a solid oak door. Above them, the storm showed little signs of abating. The Lance Corporal sighed.

"Well, the building looks solid enough. We would have the high ground, so it's a good defensive position. Doesn't hurt that it's dry too. A good place to hunker down for the night."

He scanned the surrounding area, or at least as much as the darkness would allow.

"Seems to be mostly open ground, so we'd have a clear line of sight if those bastards come at us again. There's a few pockets of trees over the far side for possible cover, but nothing to cause undue concern. I'd rather get the hell out altogether, but I reckon this is the next best thing."

O'Hagan leaned forward, eager to have his opinion heard. "Definitely a goer, Sarge. We gotta get out of this bloody weather. Fergie's plan gets my vote."

The team nodded in agreement. Under normal circumstances, his men wouldn't get a say, but lives were on the line now. They'd earned a bit of respect. No amount of training could have prepared them for this. Fergie edged the vehicle to the side of the road then carefully reversed it, facing down the slight incline so they could escape in a hurry if needs be. He switched off the engine and turned to Smudger, awaiting his orders.

"Right, lads, no more fucking around. This is about as dangerous as it gets. Fuck knows how much time we have, so let's get a bloody move on, shall we? Downs, O'Hagan – get the gear unloaded." Both men nodded.

"Fergie, first things first – it's probably a waste of time, but try and reach someone on comms; try to get the choppers out here ASAP. They won't believe shit about demons, so stow that crap, but they might shift arse for a 'homegrown terrorists'. Say whatever you have to, but try to get some air support in to rain fire on the fuckers." Fergie nodded. "Then, I want you on stag, mate. Keep yer eyes peeled and watch our backs in case those things show up. I don't want any surprises. Now, I'm gonna head up to this church and do a recce; we haven't got the time or the manpower to do a full sweep, so I'll give it the quick once-over. We can double-check once we're all inside. Here's hoping it's all clear."

Without need for further instruction, they flung open the doors and set about their tasks.

CHAPTER NINE

The noise of the heavy wooden door opening sounded cavernous within the confines of the church, despite its size. Smudger took his first step across the threshold and paused, senses struggling against the gloom. It took a few seconds for his eyes to adjust to the darkness.

He coughed slightly as a plume of dust gently wafted around him, dislodged by his sudden intrusion. The building appeared to be in a bad state of repair. It smelt of mildew and neglect. The local congregation seemed to have little use for God and his earthly representatives. The sounds of O'Hagan and Downs approaching snapped him back to the task at hand.

He edged forward, his eyes sweeping from left to right. Six shabby pews lined the room on each side. There was a crumpled copy of the bible every two feet or so, meticulously set out for the flock and rotting gently.

The church itself was small— approximately fifty-foot square by his assessment. The only other door was off to the right of the altar, directly in front of him. The cautious Marine edged his way around to the left and cleared the area hidden behind the structure.

He looked up just as O'Hagan and Downs entered the building, carrying flight cases. The Irishman sneezed loudly as he dropped his load on the floor, the impact dislodging yet more dust.

"Jesus Christ Almighty!" he exclaimed, wafting his hand in front of his face. He took in his surroundings as Downs rested his load on a pew.

"This shit-hole takes me back to my good old Catholic

days back in Belfast, so it does."

"Never had you pegged for all that fire and brimstone stuff," said Downs.

The Irishman smiled, "Pays to keep yer options open mate, wouldn't you say? Never know when you'll get a late-night sneaky visit from one of them horny priests. Or jumped by a squad of otherworldly beasties, for that matter."

Downs laughed nervously, but it wasn't really funny. Collins loomed large in their minds. Instead, they turned their attention to Smudger, who had made his way to the second door and began to work on the thick metal latch.

"Need some back-up there, Sarge?"

The sudden address made Smudger jump. He turned and glared at O'Hagan.

"I'm perfectly capable of opening a door, Marine. Now sod off and get the rest of the gear in before those bastards come back for another go!"

The Reserves turned quickly and disappeared through the front door, neither willing to push him too far.

Smudger returned his attention to the door and manipulated the handle. The door didn't budge. He grimaced and lowered his rifle to put his full body weight behind his second attempt. This time he shoulder-barged the door and, with a mournful creak, it finally gave. He promptly grabbed his rifle and swung the barrel up, ready to unload. But nothing happened, the small anteroom was void of any hostiles. He moved cautiously inside, taking in the details. To his left sat a small wooden desk, flanked by a solid-looking bookshelf which was rammed with heavy-looking books. Antique. To his right was an old chesterfield sofa, the leather cracked and worn. He entered further and glanced behind the door—it was clear. It was then that Smudger noticed another small opening, set back in the gloom beyond the sofa. He edged towards it, barrel raised.

The aperture was doorless and was no bigger than a family sized fridge, its weathered surrounds and mantle formed of heavy stone slabs, time-worn and drab. As he got closer, he could see the beginnings of a spiral stone staircase beyond, disappearing upwards. He let out a disgruntled sigh and entered the gloom.

***

Fergie tightened his jacket collar and tugged at his woollen beanie hat. He scrutinized the darkness around him once again and squinted against the harsh weather. While keeping watch, he'd shot more than a cursory glance at the blackened shapes of the gravestones. Their inscriptions would have been virtually unreadable even on the brightest of days, showing their great age as much as any date. What would their occupants have made of the events transpiring? Hell, what did he make of it all? The Scotsman snarled at himself and tried to shake these thoughts. He knew full well that dwelling on the situation was never a good thing. Not in the moment.

He had learned this the hard way through numerous tours of Iraq and Afghanistan. Desert, jungle, or urban—the location didn't matter. Distractions got you dead. You just had to accept the hand you were dealt and remain professional, ultimately letting the training take over; it was as simple as that. Fergie had walked a little way up the pathway, trying to gain a better signal. He was relieved to be out of the flood water for however brief a time. As he listened intently, tuning through the frequencies, his only irritant was the subdued shuffling of his fellow Marines, shifting the gear from the Land Rover. Their spirits seemed a little too jovial given the situation. All a front for scared little boys. He dug in, listening for any scrap of signal, and occasionally broadcasting, seeking any kind of response.

"All done," a voice announced from his rear some minutes later.

The big man turned to see Downs standing a little way down the gravel track. Beyond him, the silhouette of

O'Hagan struggled to light a cigarette in the wind. Fergie nodded and moved towards them.

"Top stuff, lads. I'm having shit-all luck at the moment. Let's get our arses inside and get this gear organised."

After shaking themselves down, they gathered around the small stack of unloaded equipment. Smudger was nowhere to be seen. The Scotsman opened the nearest flight case and admired the contents. He couldn't help but feel elated.

"I reckon this bad boy'll give those fuckers a headache if they come back!"

All three men stared lovingly at the Belgian-designed FN SAW light machine gun. Its bulky frame and vicious appearance felt somewhat reassuring.

"Right then, what else we got?" Fergie asked, lighting his roll-up. Downs bent down and flipped the security latch on the second flight case. It was full of ammo. The young Marine examined the contents, the speed of his mental arithmetic quite impressive.

"Right," he said. "By the looks of it, we've got a tad over two thousand rounds of 5.56mm for the SA80s, and that's including the surplus stuff. It may not be pretty, there might be the odd dud round, but it'll hopefully do the job. That gives us just over four hundred rounds each for our personals, but—" he gestured towards the FN, "—a hell of a lot less if we need to let rip with Ol' Dependable, here."

Fergie let out a sigh.

"Point taken. Best we pick our battles, then. No full auto unless absolutely necessary. Right, glad we got that sorted. What's in the last case?" he asked.

Once again, it was down to the youngest Marine to inspect the contents.

"If the SAW gave you a hard-on, yer gonna love this,

boys," he said, his face alight with almost religious fervour.

"Well?" O'Hagan asked impatiently.

The Scotsman shuffled forward to take in the view.

"Sweet Jesus!" O'Hagan muttered as they gathered around. "I didn't know we even had this baby. You've been holding out on us, Sarge." He looked over at the rear door, but there was no response.

"Now we're talking!" Fergie said, grinning, taking in the even bulkier frame of the L7A2 General Purpose Machine Gun. A real beast.

"How many rounds have we got for this beauty?" he demanded.

"That's the bad news," said Downs. "We've only got five hundred rounds, give or take. If I remember rightly, this thing slings six-hundred-and-fifty to a thousand rounds per minute, so we've only got a quick blast."

"ah, bollocks," O'Hagan groused, rolling his eyes. "That's hardly worth the effort."

Fergie gave him the hard stare, unimpressed by the Irishman's tone. "Maybe so, but it's all we've got. Better to have it and not need it, than need it and not have it!"

O'Hagan bobbed about awkwardly, unable to maintain eye-contact. Instead, he returned his attention to his mate and crouched down on his haunches.

"Anything else?" he asked, hoping to deflect the Scotsman's anger.

"Yep, we've got us six more grenades to add to our little shindig," said Downs.

O'Hagan slumped himself on the nearest bench and rubbed his eyes. "We could really have done with the rest of the gear from the other Rovers..."

"Be fucking grateful I split it; we could have ended up with zip!" barked Fergie, his patience all but gone. "Now stop your whining and make yourself useful. Go and find the Sarge!"

O'Hagan hopped to his feet. He gripped his weapon and started to make his way between the pews.

"What's the plan now, boss?" asked Downs, hefting his rifle.

"When the shit hits the fan, go old-school," replied Fergie. Downs nodded, eyes fixed on the mighty Scot, his eagerness evident.

"Right, young'un, first things first. I want four or five of these benches up against that front door. It isn't perfect, but at least it might slow those fuckers down." He paused to study the front aperture of the church.

"And wire up a couple of the grenades; that'll make for a nice wee surprise if they breach the perimeter. Next, I want a defensive position halfway in. We can use a couple more benches and set up the heavy artillery— hopefully, they won't get that far, but I don't want to take any chances. If they do get in, go sparingly with the rounds and pick your targets. Not suppression fire, got that?"

The kid nodded.

"OK then, let's get shit sorted."

***

Smudger had followed the staircase skyward. His rifle kept catching on the walls, God fuck it! He was surprised anyone could fit up them at all. At some points he'd been forced to turn sideways, his webbing scraping at the dirt-encrusted stonework. Once at the top, he was greeted by a thick wooden door, in relatively good repair. He tried the latch and, to his surprise, the door opened with ease. He poked his rifle through as the door swung backwards, its hinges almost silent. Something nagged at the back of his brain, but he couldn't put a finger on it. From down below, he heard the unmistakable voice of O'Hagan, calling his name. He ignored it and moved into the room, his finger resting across the trigger guard.

It was empty, he saw immediately. What a let down. No furniture, nor visible evidence of occupation. There was a small window straight ahead though, its stained-glass panels cracked and odd-looking. The damage permitted a chill breeze to scour the room. He couldn't make out the image, encrusted as it was with mould, so he moved closer. The smell was dank and disgusting. He didn't feel like touching the mould, let alone scraping it away. Instead, he peered out, looking for any sign of the enemy. The window itself was facing the front of the building, which was strange, as he hadn't noticed a second storey or a tower when they had first observed it. From his vantage point, he could see the Land Rover parked below and the ever-present stormy darkness beyond.

Cold ran through his body like a wave, breaking his composure. He held his left hand up to eye level and stood mesmerised as it began to shake uncontrollably. Smudger scrunched his eyes shut and tried to will the trembling away. Jesus, if he couldn't control his own body, how could he expect to control his men, let alone the rest of his life?

The shaking had been getting worse, progressively, over the last couple of months. Of course, he had neither sought medical attention, nor spoken of it to his squad. To his mind, if he just took a few painkillers and gritted his teeth, it would work itself out in the end. No need to make a mountain out of a molehill. And he hadn't. That was until a family member persuaded him to get himself checked out, just in case, just over a week ago. To be honest, he wished he hadn't. It was the early onset of Parkinson's disease apparently. Fucking Parkinson's. Unbelievable. Dodge bullets, IEDs and fucking sword-wielding terrorists around the world and what happens? Taken out of the game by an 'old man's' affliction—that's what he'd thought it to be, prior to diagnosis. Since then, he'd learned it could strike anyone down. It was a cruel and merciless killer. More to the point, it was incurable. He'd decided to keep it to himself. In truth, he couldn't give a fuck about his ex-wife's take on it, but Stacy, that was entirely different. She mustn't know. Not yet, anyway. He wanted to build some bridges with her before she forgot who her real dad was, before he was completely replaced. Worse still was the idea of being unable to hold her, just lying in a puddle of his own piss. No fucking way was he gonna allow that to happen.

"You OK, Sarge?"

Smudger flinched. Once again, the harsh northern Irish crow from downstairs had split the ambience. He cursed under his breath for being so jumpy, and lowered his weapon.

"Yeah, yeah. I'm OK. Just finishing up here. Why not make yourself useful and get a bloody brew on, eh?" he said, turning to face the doorway.

Smudger hadn't noticed the dark shape, watching from the shadows behind the door. He did catch a sound briefly, and began to turn, but the heavy chunk of wood struck his forehead before he could do anything else.

***

"Sarge! Sarge!"

The voice sounded distant, almost otherworldly. Deep down, it sounded familiar, but for some reason he couldn't determine where it had come from. His head hurt abominably, and his eyes ached.

"Sarge! Holy shit, you OK? You had us worried there for a minute."

Smudger blinked and looked about him and up at the beaming faces of Downs and Fergie. Everything seemed hazy and dim.

"What the hell happened?" he croaked, his head still

swimming from the blow. Fergie huffed and thumbed towards the fifth person occupying the room; a stranger. Behind them, O'Hagan stood motionless, fierce, his rifle pointing at their head.

"We got ourselves a visitor, mate, and a pretty arsey one at that."

Smudger focused on their new addition. Sat cross-legged on the floor was a skinny young man in his late twenties, his features pinched and awkward. His right eye sported a fresh bruise, presumably a gift from O'Hagan. He was dressed in mud-encrusted cargo trousers and a thick, matted jumper. A civilian, obviously. The young man squirmed, avoiding eye contact and clearly unhappy.

"Fucking fantastic," croaked Smudger. "You mean to tell me I got my ticket punched by Harry bloody Potter here?" Fergie grinned and pulled Smudger to his feet.

The sergeant cleared his throat. "How long have I been out? And, more importantly, did you manage to get anyone on comms? I could do with some good news."

Fergie shrugged. "You've only been out a few minutes. No joy with reaching anyone yet, so there's no air support en route. Downs and I have both tried to get through, but we reckon the equipment is pretty much useless. Not sure if it's the storm or the...other stuff going on. O'Hagan heard a commotion and found you on the deck with this wannabe 'bad-ass' standing over. Honestly, Shaun – a chair leg? I thought you had a tougher noggin than that. Liam gave him a quick slap, and he started to cry. I dinnae think he likes us much."

Smudger let out a raspy sigh. "Cheers, Liam."

"No worries, Sarge," came the chirpy reply.

Smudger had no intention of hurting the young man, but he didn't want him to know that. Not until he got some answers. He crouched down to the bespectacled prisoner.

"Right then, fella, just who the hell are you, and, more importantly, why did you feel the need to twat me over the head with a chair leg?" The young man lowered his head and turned away, embarrassed and afraid. Smudger poked him in the chest but felt a sense of remorse as he watched him recoil. He decided to take a gamble.

"You thought I was one of those things, didn't you? That's why you clocked me."

"You've seen them too?" he croaked, hopefully. "The...things."

Smudger nodded slowly, happy to be proven right.

"We were attacked a few miles down the road by a shitload of them. Managed to take a few of them out. Fragged their leader."

"You killed her? Are you sure she's dead? Where is the body?"

Smudger swallowed hard. "I said fragged. From what I saw, I doubt she's dead. Now—How did you know it was a 'her'? Spill the beans, kid, because I'm gonna lose my shit pretty damn soon. What the fuck is happening?"

The young man found the courage to hold his gaze for a moment. "You wouldn't believe me if I told you; you'd think I was crazy—everybody else does."Smudger bent down and placed his hands on the lad's shoulders, squeezing a little for emphasis.

"Look, mate, we've witnessed some pretty messed-up shit tonight, and I've lost a good man—a friend. My lads are strung out, hungry, and living on their nerves, so if you can shed any light on what's going on out there, we need to hear it."

The man nodded and sucked in a deep breath.

"My name is Jonathan Brewer and I have more than a passing interest in ancient pagan folklore. I've had books published on the topic. The woman you 'fragged'" he drew the quotation marks with his fingers, "is a Huldra."

Smudger didn't flinch. "And what, pray tell, is a Huldra?"

"One of the 'Hidden Folk.' Mythological beings who dwell in the forests, streams, and caves of Norse, Germanic, and English folklore. The Huldra are supposed to be kind, friendly even, if offerings are left and they're treated with respect. But...well, I guess they haven't had much of that for a long time now."

"OK," said Smudger, "let's say we take you at your word. How the hell do you know so much?—and what the hell are all those other things with her? Trolls, Dwarves, Demons? I'm pretty sure there were a few men in there, too." The seated prisoner shrugged his shoulders.

"To answer your questions, I know what I'm talking about because I've studied this stuff for years. The creatures are all of the things you've said and then some. They are all part of what legends call 'The Wild Hunt', and from what I understand, there is absolutely nothing we can do to stop it. Worse, if you die by the hunt, you get dragged from the grave to join it. That's what'll happen to your friend. Fallen comrades become the enemy of the living."

Downs raised his hand and coughed.

"I thought that was just some Glastonbury shite. Isn't it supposed to be all demon hounds, dead warriors and fairies, like...riding through the sky, taking souls?"

A wry smile touched the corner of the prisoner's mouth. "That's just Christian scaremongering, their way of dominating indigenous faiths and its followers. In Scandinavian lore, The Wild Hunt is led by the god Odin; in Anglo Saxon chronicles, it's Woden. Depending on which Northern European culture we're talking about, they all have their variants, but one thing they all agree on is that there is no way to stop it. It has always happened and will continue long after we're dust. All we can do is to hide and hope to avoid their attention."

"A bit bloody late for that, eh, lads?" quipped Smudger. "Hang on a minute though, are you saying that Huldra thing isn't their leader?"

The prisoner shook his head. "Not the leader, no, but a catalyst for the hunt to begin. A general of sorts. Sometimes Odin or the primary deity appears in the tales, other times, not. There are no set rules governing The Hunt, only a blood-lust."

Smudger thought back to their encounter of the road and pondered that one for a moment. Humanity may not have learned the rules, but there was some organising force there, holding the horde back, testing the Marines for weaknesses. It wasn't just some wild stampede, even after the grenade. Something else to worry about, then. Something bigger. More powerful. Fuck.

"All right, so you're a boffin," he growled. "I'll buy it. What are you doing out here. School outing, or what?"

Brewer shook his head. "I'm not an academic as such – I actually work at a supermarket in Glastonbury – but I do spend my free time researching the Pagan history of Somerset, and the Vikings of course. It's a passion of mine, my life's work really."

Fergie shook his head, unsure if he had heard correctly. "The Vikings? They didn't get down this far, did they? I thought they stayed up north. York and all that."

Brewer chuckled, finding the soldier's lack of knowledge amusing.

"As with anything relating to history, there are always conflicting stories, not to mention new hypotheses. The history books tell us that some elements of The Great Heathen Army passed through the Somerset Levels, hunting the English King, Alfred, so, whilst they didn't lay down roots, they were most definitely in the area. But I have another theory as to why they ventured this far west."

"Well," said Smudger, "what's the theory?"

Brewer rubbed his hands together with childlike excitement.

"Firstly, you have to take into consideration that to these people, in this moment in history, Somerset was on the very edge of the unknown, the furthest reaches of Wessex: mightiest of the Anglo-Saxon kingdoms. To the Norsemen, it represented, to some degree, the furthest point from their homeland. To the vast majority, the south-west of what we call 'England' was nothing but a barren, marshy wasteland, of no real importance. In other words, they could get about unmolested. I think they brought something to these shores: something they desperately wanted to get rid of. The 'hunt' for Alfred was probably cooked up by locals trying to understand or explain their presence."

Smudger was starting to get the gist.

"And you think the thing they wanted to get rid of was this Huldra bitch, yeah?"

"Indeed, that's exactly what I'm saying. Think about it—what better place to banish some ancient evil blighting their lands? With luck it would stay buried, but if it did escape, there's a whole country full of Christians to slaughter its way through before it could ever hope to return. No record, no evidence. It's perfect." The young man's story sounded nuts, but with everything he and his men had witnessed, it was as good an explanation as any.

"OK, let's pretend for a minute that you are correct, that still doesn't explain how the hell they managed to stop her back then with nothing but swords and axes."

Brewer got to his feet and reached under his woollen jumper. The four Marines watched silently as he produced a small bundle of rags. He unwrapped it carefully and held his hands out for the team to inspect its contents.

"Because, my good fellow, they had this."

All four men stared at the rusted, barely recognisable spearhead. Its edges had dulled over time but it still looked formidable. Smudger leaned closer, his curiosity peaked.

"Where the hell did you get that thing? You nick it from a museum, or what?"

"I most certainly did not!" snapped Brewer, deeply offended by the notion.

Smudger held his hands up in mock surrender.

"OK, OK, just joking, relax," he offered by way of apology. "Then where did you get it, or is that classified information?"

Brewer settled down and lowered his voice.

"Over the years, I read a few scattered accounts that the Great Heathen Army had employed the services of a Gothi —a Norse holy man, practitioner of ancient magics and communicator with the dead. Someone who would have been taken very seriously in the Viking age, and who had the power to defeat, or in this instance, to bind the evil plaguing his kinsfolk. According to my research, he accomplished this by impaling the Huldra with a Galdr spear. The binding complete, he then buried her in a secret place, there to rest forever."

"A what spear?" asked Downs.

"Galdr. The rune magic of the ancestors. According to the Norsemen, each rune could be sung, and when done so out loud, it released the power of the rune into the surrounding place, people, or objects, imbuing them with magical properties."

"Gothic bloke and fairy tales. Fucking splendid," Fergie replied, taking a long drag on his roll-up.

"I really can't be arsed with this shite anymore," grunted O'Hagan. "Nobody ever said I would have to lay the smack down on Tinkerbell."

Smudger stretched his arms, his shoulder aching from the constant cold and the damp. He glared at his men in turn, each absorbing this information.

"Right, lads!" O'Hagan and Downs looked at their CO.

"Sir," they replied as one.

"Get yer arses downstairs and finish off the defences, we've been tossing it off up here for too long. I've got a feeling those bastards will be back sooner rather than later, so hop to it!" Both men saluted and made their way downstairs. Smudger cleared his throat.

"How long does this Wild Hunt last?"

Brewer shrugged.

"No one knows. Supposed historical accounts don't give much indication, only that it happens at night and during midwinter."

"Just at night? Well that's something. Once the storm ends we should be able to get out by chopper, that's assuming the comms come back online. Otherwise it's a long wet walk tomorrow."

"How did you get that spear, anyway?" asked Smudger.

Brewer's mood seemed to change, apparently reluctant to answer the question. He mopped his brow.

"I had been working on a theory that the burial site was located somewhere on the Somerset levels, and over several painstaking years narrowed it down. I sold my house and used all my savings to pay a local workman to dig trial trenches in areas I thought would bear fruit. Over the last three years, we'd found nothing, but that changed yesterday. He found a large grave with evidence of what appeared to be broken Viking glassware and several shattered sword blades. He kept digging, and lo and behold, he found the spear—"

"—And?" Fergie interrupted.

"That's when I told him I would double his money if he kept digging the site," sighed Brewer. Well, undoubtedly he disturbed the Huldra's resting place. Earlier this evening, I saw an explosion of green light, and then those things started to appear; it was the catalyst for the Wild Hunt to begin. I wasn't at the dig, you understand, but back at my campervan, a little way down the road. And that's where I saw her."

"Did she come after you?"

"No. It was horrible, though. She just stood staring at me, smiled, and then vanished—right in front of my eyes."

Fergie began to laugh bitterly. "So it's your fault she's up to her old tricks, then? Cheers, pal."

Brewer lowered his head. "I believe so."

Smudger hefted his weapon.

"It doesn't matter who started this, or even why. Let's just make it through the night in one piece." He worked the charging handle. "And if she gets in the way, we'll put her down. Her and her boss. Any means necessary."

No sooner had he spoken than the night came alive – the deafening crack of an explosion. Not thunder. Not this time. The sky and room around them was illuminated by a blinding orange-and-white flash. Smudger and Fergie bolted to the window, their weapons at the ready. Smudger strained against the glass, finding vantage points around the mould, peering at different angles, eyes scanning the terrain below. The burning wreckage of the Land Rover below lit up the grasslands nearby, raging in the wind and rain.

Slowly, as their eyes adjusted, they began to see signs of movement. From the darkness and surrounding shadows, twisted figures began to appear.

Fergie huffed. "Persistent bitch, ain't she?"

As they watched, the Huldra paused and raised her face to the window. "Oh, bollocks," muttered Smudger as the fiend smiled.

And with a single hand gesture, she set the horde loose.

"GO!" Smudger yelled as the creatures surged forward . The three men bolted through the doorway and raced down the stairs. The church was rocked once again by another explosion as Smudger reached the bottom step, stumbling backwards.

"What the fuck was that?" growled Smudger as he dragged himself to his feet. "The Land Rover's already gone up."

"Grenades!" came the raspy response from Fergie. Both men staggered to their feet and powered through to the church, their rifles at their shoulders, accompanied by the all-too-familiar crackle of gunfire.

"They're inside!" Fergie yelled.

CHAPTER TEN

It was a war-zone. The heavy oak door was shattered, its blackened remnants littering the floor. The ceiling directly above the archway was ablaze, flames licking at the rotting beams and plaster. Smudger scanned the scorched brickwork and coughed on the acrid smoke. He waved a hand in front of his face and quickly surveyed the area, momentarily lingering on the swarm of otherworldly creatures now crashing through the entrance. The scene around him moved in slow motion, adrenaline giving him all the time he needed to act. The snap of gunfire lent rhythm to the scene as Downs and O'Hagan battled to stem the tide. High-pitched screams from the creatures as bullets entered flesh. The stench of gunpowder and blood saturated his senses. Fergie moved past him, rifle at his shoulder, spitting forth its deadly load.

"Smudger!"

He snapped out of his trance, levelled his weapon and let loose a volley of lead. Behind him, Brewer ducked down, transfixed by fear, as the four soldiers fought for their lives. Smudger and Fergie edged forward, their arc of fire sweeping from left to right, peppering the wall of monsters with high-velocity bullets. Below them, crouched behind stacked pews, O'Hagan and Downs kept their fire focused on the crowded doorway as fresh waves crawled over the mounting dead, their eyes aglow with hatred. The beasts were unrelenting.

O'Hagan sensed something off to his right and saw a black shadow, cast across the rubble and masonry. He tried to yell a warning the others but the words barely squeaked out.

"What the sweet fuck?"

Five Vikings appeared in the doorway, their hulking frames jostling to force their way into the building.

"Get down!" Fergie screamed as the first warrior flung its arm forward, releasing a rusted and savage-looking axe. Smudger had just enough time to dive to his left, slamming into a pile of broken wood and brick. The colossal weapon spun past his head and slammed into the stone wall behind him with a resounding crack. The impact sent a cloud of dust and fine debris into the air. Fergie could only gape as his friend staggered to his feet, his face ashen.

Before either man could engage this latest threat, leaping with surprising agility over the blockage in the doorway, the building shook with a new and devastating noise. Downs had opened up with the belt-fed machine gun, a crazed smile on his face.

"Fuck you, you Wild Cunts!" he screamed, cutting the warriors in half, reducing their un-mortal remains to a mist. Downs pulled the weapon back into his shoulder and kept his finger on the trigger long after the final bullets were spent. It was a scene of utter carnage. Smudger levelled his rifle and moved swiftly to Downs, slapping him on his shoulder, telling him to ease off. Fergie moved position as O'Hagan got to his feet, and together they moved towards the open doorway, their hearts racing, the report of the heavy weapon still ringing painfully in their ears.

"O'Hagan, on me!" cried Fergie as the Irishman moved swiftly to his side. They pressed forward, their rifles now sweeping the gaping void for further threats. Behind them, Smudger and Downs got to their feet, Downs ditching the heavy machine gun, now useless, and retrieving his rifle. Eyes wide, he nodded at his CO, then turned to cover his comrades at the doorway.

"How's it looking?" Smudger called after them. O'Hagan was the first to turn, his face a little grey.

"There's bloody loads of them, Sarge, no chance of us getting out this way!"

"Fergie, what's your take?"

"What he said. They ain't moving though; they're just standing there, watching. If I had to take a guess, I reckon they're waiting for us to come out guns blazing – Butch and Sundance style. Easier tae get us out there in the open. They may be ugly but they ain't stupid."

"Bollocks!" snapped Smudger, trying to think of a Plan B. But Fergie was right. There was no other exit. He turned to Brewer, who looked frankly terrified.

"Well, have you got any bright ideas, boffin?" he asked, bitterly. Brewer shifted his weight and grimaced. "I do, actually."

Smudger glared. "Well? Care to share?"

"You aren't going to like it," Brewer added, apologetically. "You see, um, this main building is pretty damn old. 12th Century as a ballpark date, though the rear section, complete with the stairwell and upper floor, is a later addition. 18th Century, probably." Smudger huffed and tapped his rifle, his annoyance obvious.

"Great. And how exactly does that help?"

"Well, as we have seen," continued Brewer, "it takes an awful lot of firepower to make the smallest dent in this older structure, but—" Smudger was hit with the sudden realisation of what the man was proposing. It was so obvious, he almost felt embarrassed. He smiled ruefully and let the man finish.

"—the rear, which is younger and less well-made, is a damn sight easier to breach."

Smudger playfully patted Brewer on the cheek then turned to address his men.

"Right then, new plan: who's got the grenades?"

O'Hagan reached over his shoulder and tossed a small rucksack to his CO. Smudger caught it and spun on his heels.

"Keep an eye on those bastards. Try to give me three minutes!" he bellowed as he headed through the doorway, Brewer following closely behind.

Once in the back room, Smudger checked the walls and addressed his companion.

"OK then, Mr Brewer. Where exactly should we blow it without bringing the whole place down on our heads?"

The academic adjusted his glasses and, with a half-hearted gesture, pointed to the area behind the Chesterfield sofa.

"My best guess would be there. The re-enforced mantel of the stairwell and doorway should be strong enough to withstand the blast internally, yet the wall weak enough to break through"

Smudger smiled darkly at him.

"Ain't no room for *should be* in this game, mate. You better be sure, coz if you ain't, we're all dead men."

Brewer didn't flinch.

"If it doesn't work, we are all dead men anyway, are we not?"

"Fair point, Mr Smart Arse." He tugged open the bag and dug his hand in, pulling three grenades free. Then, after a moment's pause, he retrieved a fourth.

"Fuck it. Like you said, we're all dead men anyway, eh?" He was still smiling as he set then up, fixing them in place and attaching a length of wire to the pins. They all had to go at once. Brewer swallowed hard.

"Should I alert the others?" Brewer asked, his voice betraying his fear. Smudger slung his weapon, yanked the sofa from its position, and placed it as a shelter. He shot his companion a serious glare.

"Yeah, go get them; tell them to let loose a few rounds to show them we're still in the fight, then tell them to get in here, double-time."

***

It was O'Hagan who first noticed the flashing lights in the distance, the neon blue strobe cutting through the storm. Fergie held his hand to his face, his skin stinging with the icy bite of the wind.

"You've gotta be bloody joking. Is that the Fire Brigade?"

The approaching vehicle was a couple of clicks south-east of their position; given the terrain, weather and estimated speed, Fergie reasoned that their ETA was five minutes, possibly less. A sudden sense of panic washed over him.

"Oh shit!" Fergie exclaimed. The horde had also started to take notice, their numbers now swelling from the darkness and turning towards the lights.

"We've gotta warn them!" he yelled above the wind. "They've no idea what they're walking into!"

O'Hagan nodded, patted his weapon, and both men began to fire. The sound and muzzle-flashes should alert the firemen, and if it didn't, at least they'd be taking out some more of the horde. Once again, the night erupted with a salvo of semi-automatic fire, their rounds carving into the unmissable, innumerable foe. Fergie briefly checked the location of the emergency vehicle and his heart sank. The damned thing had made better time than he'd first thought.

"Fergie?" The Lance Corporal heard his name and glanced at O'Hagan who was busy pointing towards the horrors below.

"What the...?" he croaked, as the creatures retreated silently into the surrounding deluge, their forms melting into the floodwaters and half-submerged vegetation.

"Fucking marvellous, what the hell are they doing now?" O'Hagan asked nervously, backing up a touch, his rifle still trained on the rapidly emptying area.

"I don't know, mate," said Fergie, shaking his head, "but I sure as hell don't like it."

"Fergie! O'Hagan!"

Both men turned to see the hunched frame of Brewer, standing a little way behind them—one hand to his mouth, the other struggling to keep his glasses in place.

"What?" snapped Fergie, not wanting to engage. "I'm a bit fucking busy, here!"

The academic shifted uncomfortably under the man's angry stare.

"Sarge says to let them have a few bursts then back inside, double-time. We've got a plan!"

"*We've* got a plan?" he repeated vehemently, his disdain evident. Brewer nodded, then exclaimed and pointed down the hill behind them. Both Marines spun back around to see the fire engine pulling up at the base of the hill. No sooner had it engaged the air-brakes than the cab doors were flung open, allowing six firemen out, bowed against the wind. The three men watched in disbelief as the commander began to wade towards them while his colleagues set about retrieving equipment from various lockers, entirely oblivious to their danger. Fergie stepped forward and began frantically waving his arms. "No! Get back! Stay in the truck!" His words vanished in the howling wind and the firefighter kept on coming. Fergie moved another couple of feet, his weapon now raised, the safety off, hoping the sight of it would give the man pause.

O'Hagan yelled something wild and despairing as the night exploded in barbarity. The seething mass of creatures had reappeared, their chaotic forms leaping from the blackened shallows, limbs wreathed in wisps of green iridescence. Fergie couldn't breathe, his senses were besieged as the creatures enveloped their would-be saviours, like a swarm of hungry locusts.

"Noooooo!" Fergie cried through clenched teeth as the horde eviscerated, then devoured the unarmed rescuers. He took another step forward, desperate to enter the fray, but the Irishman caught hold of his arm and held him back. Despite the raging storm, he could hear their muffled screams, but only for the briefest of moments. Then they turned their attention to their primary foes, a thousand yellow eyes seeking out their prey. As a united front, they surged forward.

The speed of the creatures' attack was dizzying, and they had little choice but to run—their boots, thick with mud, sliding on the saturated earth. Behind them, the creatures gained ever more ground, the air alive with shrills and the excited chatter of the Hunt.

The three men powered through the church doorway to the welcome sight of Marine Downs, his weapon raised. Fergie threw Brewer to one side, O'Hagan leapt to the other, and Downs let loose at their pursuers. The Marines scrambled down the sides of the church towards the back room as Downs emptied his magazine then, spinning on his heels, he followed. Even as he ran, a familiar shape caught his eye, half-covered by bricks and hellish body parts.

"'Avin' that!" he quipped to himself, scooping up the SAW light machine gun. He had only managed another four steps, spinning to keep his balance, when the church was rocked by another enormous explosion.

CHAPTER ELEVEN

Libby Hooper was a good girl. Her mum told her so, repeatedly. Her dad used to say she was 'eight going on twenty' but that was before he'd left for work—two years earlier—and never came back. It was nothing to do with the fact that Libby was different, mum said, but she still harboured secret suspicions that being 'special' wasn't something to be proud of. The other children made it sound like a bad thing. Like she was a disease.

Having few friends and living in such an isolated place, Libby had learned to find solace in the written word. Tall tales transported her to distant shores, far from those who enjoyed cruelty. Stories of handsome knights and dragons, detectives and adventures fuelled her passion; her explorations were limitless. She had decided—and took great delight in announcing—that when she grew up, she would be an author, to help others, as books had helped her. Mum encouraged her passion, of course. She used to tell her that she was a star, burning so brightly it made the other kids jealous. She had even painted the night sky on her bedroom ceiling. Every night, she would fall asleep, her mind adrift among a thousand stars.

She had always been close to her mum, and she used to think she had a special connection with her dad, but it would appear she had been wrong about that part. Maybe one day she would track him down and ask, but for now, it was better to keep quiet. She didn't want to upset her mum. For about a year after her dad had left, she would hear her mum crying when she thought she was alone. Sometimes Libby would give her mum some space, other times she would simply give her a hug, neither of them saying a word.

Libby took a tiny swig from her water bottle then replaced it in her backpack, nestled between her torch and three chocolate bars. Mum had left the house a little over an hour ago to search for their dog, who had run off into the storm. Titan must have seen something and decided to investigate, no doubt protecting his family. Such a loyal dog! Libby had offered to help but had been reassured, and asked to stay put. Not to leave the house under any circumstance until mum returned. Of course, being the good girl she was, she did as she was told. But it had been a long time now. An awfully long time.

Libby stood by the back door now, the wind and the rain battering the glass and shaking the frame. The house itself was in darkness save for two candles on the kitchen table, their flickering flames casting eerie shadows across the walls and the cupboards. She zipped up her storm-proof jacket and tucked in her chin, hoping this protection would keep whatever was lurking in the shadows at bay. Her silent prayers were a shield to protect her mum and a request for Titan to return unharmed.

She was worried. Desperately so. Just after her mum had left, Libby began to see shapes stalking through the rain-scarred darkness, emerging from the shadows, moving past the house and along the flooded road.

To ten-year-old Libby, these shapes were not only unusual but scary, like the creatures in the books her mum liked to read. The books she wasn't supposed to touch. Having been born and raised on the Somerset Levels, she knew what sheep, horses and goats looked like, even at night, silhouetted and strange, but these were so very different. There was something in the way they moved that gave the impression they wanted to hurt you—not because they were defending themselves or that they were hungry, but because they enjoyed it. She'd only seen humans move like that before, but the size and shapes didn't match. No. She was convinced now. They were monsters.

Another ten minutes passed, during which she heard

Wild Hunters

loud bangs in the distance and saw bright flashes across the fields, up towards the old church. And still her mother did not return, though the flow of horrid shapes had dwindled and stopped. Libby moved cautiously to the window, edging along the wall to peep out. She rubbed the moisture from the glass and scanned the darkness. It was a risky thing to do but she had no choice—she had to be sure before she acted. She had never been so brave. Satisfied, she moved back to the table and retrieved her backpack. She checked the contents one last time: two bottles of water, three chocolate bars, a torch, a thin jumper, and a box of matches. She clucked her tongue. Something was missing. She slid the cutlery drawer open and pulled out a vegetable knife. The sharpest they had. *Every hero needs a magical sword*, she mused. She tucked it inside her pack with her supplies, secured it, then slung it over her shoulder.

After blowing out the candles, she stood motionless by the back door. She checked her shoelaces and jacket zip, then finally pulled up her hood. Like any good literary heroine, she would have to take matters into her own hands. She had no other choice.

Libby's small, detached cottage had no real neighbours to speak of, the nearest being over two miles away. the old church was closer, and higher up; a good place to look out across the area to try to spot her mum. She was confident of reaching her destination, although it would mean she'd have to follow the river, and that was usually off-limits. Still, mum wasn't to know. She just had to be careful, was all.

Libby had a wobble at the thought, and suddenly doubted her course of action. Would a good girl do something her mum had specifically told her not to do? She shook her head and gritted her teeth. No—but what if mum was hurt somewhere and needed help? She wouldn't be *able* to tell her it was alright now. To come and find her. Libby's mind was made up and her plan simple. She would make her way to the old church and the source of the noises and lights. Hopefully, the people there were nice and

95

would help her find her mum. And Titan. After a final look around she took a deep breath and walked out into the storm.

CHAPTER TWELVE

Fergie let out a shallow gasp of relief when the grime-covered figure of Smudger appeared in the doorway of the back room, rifle raised, beckoning him in. It was then Fergie caught sight of the great hole in the wall. He ducked straight through it, with Downs close behind, eager to escape the killing grounds of the church.

"Took yer bloody time, didn't ya?" Smudger announced as the Marines passed him. For a split second, he couldn't see the others, the rain lashing hard against his exposed face. He winced as he tried to focus, his lungs screaming for fresh oxygen. He levelled his rifle and looked about him, probing every little shadow, convinced that the shadows harboured yet more unseen atrocities. Downs had no such thoughts. He simply fled. As Fergie's night vision returned, he noticed Brewer and O'Hagan further down a gravel track, at the end of which was a large structure, flanked by a small gathering of trees.

"Come on, old-timer, move your arse! We ain't got all day!" he bellowed as his dust-covered friend cleared the building. It was then the Scotsman noticed movement from within. The monsters had wasted no time following. At a glance, there seemed to be fifty or so creatures emerging, but that wasn't the thing that worried him—it was the ones stalking around the building from both sides.

Fergie dropped to one knee and fired. There was a deafening snap, a blinding flash, the savage bite of recoil. The night came alive once more with the nightmarish screams of the enemy as his projectiles found their mark, tearing through flesh and bone.

As Smudger raced towards his friend, a scrawny elfish creature sprung at him from the side, cat-like and quick.

The Marine recoiled as the thing lashed out, its features pointed and wicked, its fingers topped with vicious talons. Smudger instinctively span to the side and felt himself toppling over, his boot tangled in weeds. There was nothing he could do to stop his fall, and with an explosive splash, he crashed into a waterlogged ditch. The spindly thing made a dance of its hunt with two graceful corrections, then leapt upon his chest, its snapping teeth inches from his face as he tried to hold it back. It lashed out with its formidable claws, savagely slicing the Sergeant's cheeks and upper torso. Smudger recoiled, bellowing, and blood gushed freely from the wounds, his eye sockets pooling with red.

Fergie swallowed hard and raced towards his stricken brother, the abomination whooping with delight as it rained down blow after punishing blow. Behind it, gleefully creeping, four other atrocities looking to feed. With a deafening roar, he fired four shots in quick succession, guided by instinct and muscle memory. Without missing his stride, Fergie spun the rifle in his hands and swung it with all his strength. The head of creature atop Smudger snapped back and to the side, its neck cracking, expression frozen in shock. It fell limply to the side, face down in the filth. Smudger sat up, frantically wiped his eyes, trying to clear his vision, but no sooner had he done so, they were attacked again.

In a twisted ball of limbs and claws, they fought this second wave, pummelled and pinned in the stinking ditch. As they struggled amid the flailing claws and crushing weight, their bodies and will succumbing, Smudger made one last valiant effort. He rolled across his friend, acting as a barrier to shield Fergie from the worst of their depredations. The big man could imagine every slash, every bite and gouge endured, yet Smudger did not yield. All he could do was watch helplessly as his CO and closest friend was ripped to shreds, his world reduced to a sea of crimson and clawing mud.

Fergie felt Smudger go limp, the dead weight compressing his own body further into the mud. He tried to push upwards but he just didn't have the strength. The awful realization came upon him that his friend's lifeless body was the only thing preventing the creatures getting to him, compounded his descent to a guilt-driven purgatory.

He gripped him all the tighter and peered past, certain his end had come, when he noticed something strange high above. It was bright, a searing streak of orange light. The spectre was quickly followed by a raspy explosion and an even bigger flash of light, at which the creatures reared backwards, their throaty screams evidence of some unknown, yet welcome assailant.

They began to retreat as a second streak hurtled by, followed promptly by a third. Fergie pushed with everything he had and was finally afforded a glimmer of hope as Smudger's body began to shift. He pushed for a third time and felt a wave of relief as his friend's body fell to the side.

With aching limbs, he began to drag himself to his feet as Downs, Brewer and O'Hagan threw another well-aimed volley of Molotov cocktails, the crude projectiles exploding amongst the fleeing creatures.

"Come on, Fergie, no time to toss it off, fucking move it!" O'Hagan roared as he scooped up his rifle and staggered towards his companions, bedraggled and battered. He eyed his companions mournfully.

"Smudger, he's..." O'Hagan nodded and Downs slapped him on the shoulder.

"We know. Come on, let's get the fuck out of here before those things regroup."

Fergie limped down the gravel path towards the academic, who was frantically waving his arms for speed. To his rear, Downs whooped with delight as one last, well-aimed cocktail erupted, sending a plume of smoke into the sky. Fergie managed a fleeting glance over his shoulder, catching sight of a pair of creatures helplessly flailing their limbs, their foul flesh soaked with liquid fire.

It was as if that single act provided a momentary sense of reassurance, the licking flames a blazing barrier between them and their relentless pursuers; a glimmer of hope in the darkness. They came to a halt at the end of the track, nestled among trees. Fergie sucked in a series of painful breaths, his lungs and ribs still screaming from the assault.

To his left was a waterway, approximately thirty feet wide. Whatever banks usually channelled this river they had clearly been broken by the rising floodwaters. Beyond the far shore was an expanse of flooded peat bog, its bleak vastness interspersed with a few densely-packed thickets. They most definitely didn't want to be caught out there, in the open.

The waterway ran parallel to the wooden barn to his right, its double doors flung wide open, next to which sat a large, antiquated fuel tank. It didn't look to be in the best state of repair, its metal pitted and edged with patches of rust. Presumably the source of his resourceful squad's bomb-making supplies.

Fergie stepped forward and squinted into the gloom of the structure. Within, he thought he could make out the familiar shape of a waterwheel turning steadily in it's channel towards the rear of the building. Power for machinery. And where there was machinery, there was sure to be tools.

"What's the plan then, lads?" Downs asked between heavy breaths, his hands resting on his knees. O'Hagan raised his hand and pointed to the far side of the waterway, where a small Rigid Inflatable Boat was moored, half-tucked behind a makeshift jetty.

"That RIB's our ticket out of here, fellas. Probably belonged to the local waterways agency. Reckon it belongs to Her Majesty's Royal Marines now, though."

"Blinding, mate, nice one." said Fergie. "You reckon that thing will take all four of us?"

O'Hagan shrugged. "I'd have preferred a Sunseeker with a fully-stocked bar, but let's give it a try."

Fergie nodded in agreement.

"Right lads, re-load, check yer gear, and let's get wet."

It was Brewer who was the first to drag himself into the boat, swiftly followed by Downs. Once settled, both men turned to help Fergie and O'Hagan. The Irishman swiftly moved to the outboard motor and began to prime the fuel line. Downs and the Scotsman took position and trained their freshly loaded weapons in the direction of the barn and the church. There was no way this was over. O'Hagan cheered in relief as the engine spluttered into life with a high-pitched whine.

"Uh. Guys," Downs said, with growing panic. "Contact right. Move!" There on the bank, standing in perfect formation, were half a dozen apparitions. Viking bowmen, their bodies little more than wisps of vapour, yet their features unmistakable. Barbaric. At their feet were flaming staves, thrust into the ground, pointing outward. They burned a vivid green.

"You gotta be fucking kidding me—" yelled O'Hagan, clocking the threat, even as the phantoms loosed a volley.

"Incoming!" Fergie called as the ancient artillery fell about them. The Scotsman kept his head down but he heard a scream from behind him. Brewer slumped forward, struck in the shoulder. He looked like he was about to be sick, or faint maybe. Nothing anyone could do about that right now. Fortunately, the only other arrows to have found a target lay embedded in the engine cover or the solid rubber seating. Downs cast off and O'Hagan gunned the engine as the viking nocked once more, and it powered forward as they loosed, overshooting the boat by several feet.

Nobody noticed the great hand which had emerged from below to grip the boat until the rest of the creature burst forth, grabbing hold of Fergie from behind and toppling him overboard. Downs was the first to react; he shifted his body weight and lunged, desperate to snatch hold of Fergie's sodden hand, even as he disappeared beneath the surface, into the murky depths.

CHAPTER THIRTEEN

London – Undisclosed Location

The luxurious yet sparsely furnished office was dark but for the illumination from the computer screen. Sir Malcolm Hawker sat back in his leather office chair, cupping a half-filled whiskey tumbler, the ice cubes clinking the glass as he sipped the fiery liquid.

He turned his attention to the large panoramic window, the cascade of city lights blurred by the torrential downpour. He had, from this position, kept studious vigil for many a year.. Some might say he was a guardian of sorts for those who had little knowledge of how the world really worked. However, it had, to some degree, become a prison of his own making. A cell of tempered glass, steel, and concrete, from which there was no escaping. Yet, despite such tribulations, having his office in such a lofty position had its perks. During his tenure, especially during the summer months, he was beguiled by the urban sunsets, the constant wisp of industrial haze belched forth by those far below, each going about their tiny lives. He marvelled at how they could be so blissfully unaware of the stream of horrors threatening their very existence.

Despite the summer's charms, the current season was more to his liking. The winter had its own beauty. The bleak, soothing darkness kept him safely in the shadows. His work was best carried out away from prying eyes; to cast a light upon his profession would have ramifications few could comprehend. The fact was that if those outside these four walls were to learn what resided in the dark, they too would succumb to its ravenous appetite.

He took another hefty swig, savouring the taste, then

gently rested the glass on his desk, as information scrolled endlessly across his computer screen. He stretched his neck to one side and massaged his temples, head throbbing with the beginnings of yet another crushing headache. Of course, he was used to it, for *it* always happened this way. The sore limbs, followed by the migraine, culminating in the catatonic dream-state through which he gained his insight. The price for enlightenment was steep, but it was a price he would willingly pay if it meant keeping the upper hand.

His mobile phone chirped. He smiled at the number displayed on the screen and jabbed the button to answer.

"Yes?"

"Sir Malcolm, sorry to disturb you at this hour, but we have a somewhat alarming development, of which I am sure you would wish to be informed.'

Hawker relaxed into his chair.

"Go ahead. What calamity has befallen us now? I trust it isn't anything to do with the Isle of Skye incident? It was my understanding that that had been properly dealt with."

There was a short pause. The caller cleared his throat.

"Well, yes sir. As far as I am aware, that has been dealt with. However, it would appear we have lost contact with our asset in the West Country. According to our last communications, something has been, how can I put it? 'Released.' And it is currently loose on the Somerset Levels. I'm afraid this is a level-two incursion."

"I see. Contained, or is there a significant flight risk?"

There was silence from the other end.

"Should we be concerned at this point?"

"Unsure at this time, sir. We do know that the weather is playing a significant part but it is, to the best of our knowledge, working in our favour. The entire area is cut off.

In fact, even the emergency services are unable to reach certain areas. However, we do have a specialist two-man OPS team moving in to assess and relay real-time intelligence."

"What's the estimated fallout regarding civilian casualties? Witnesses to the event?"

"We estimate no more than a handful, but..."

Hawker tensed and leaned forward, taking hold of his tumbler.

"But *what*, Mr Upton? Don't be coy, spit it out, man. We haven't got all night."

"Well, sir, earlier this evening, our tech team intercepted some localised military chatter. It seems that some local Reservists happened to be in the area. Royal Marines. Some sort of exercise, apparently. Once the red warning was issued, they were ordered in by their superiors to offer assistance and evacuate the civilians. Nothing of real concern, but I thought you should be informed nonetheless."

"Mm-hmm, thank you, Mr Upton. Not an ideal situation, I'm sure you would agree. Am I correct in presuming this contingent of military personnel is without due clearance? And do we know how long they have been stomping about the hot zone? More to the point, have they made contact with the anomaly?"

"I will find out, sir, and report back with haste."

"Thank you. And if I may impose on you further, please obtain the personnel files for every man in that unit. Local yokels we can deal with. The great British public would take a little more notice of a war hero if they decide to go running their mouths off."

"Of course, Sir Malcolm. I understand. May I just add that the board does think it prudent to scramble a Tactical Reaction Team. We can have them lay-up at our airfield, from which they can be on-site via RNAS Yeovilton within twenty minutes. At the very least, they would be nearby for our asset extraction."

Hawker rubbed his forehead. His headache was getting worse.

"Fine. Have a team on stand-by. At the very least it will be an extraction, at worst, a clean-up..."

"Thank you, sir."

"Oh, and Mr Upton..."

"Yes, sir?"

"May I suggest that these Reservists also disappear amid the confusion?"

"Of course, sir. That goes without saying."

CHAPTER FOURTEEN

He was going in, and there was no way of stopping it. All Fergie could do was snatch a lungful of air as he was dragged under, the foul-tasting water washing over him as he closed his eyes. The last thing he saw was the look of horror on his teammates' faces as he flew backwards. He struggled, desperately trying to break free, his lungs screaming under the strain and the rapid descent. He forced open his eyes, his vision blurred by the filth and the swirl of a thousand bubbles as his body thrashed wildly. He lashed out instinctively with a heavy boot—and to his relief, felt the grip loosen. He kicked out again, spurred on by success and desperation, and this time felt the grip break altogether. He didn't bother to look below, kicking out and up towards the surface, on the very edge of succumbing to a watery end. Air first, fight after.

The Scotsman coughed and spluttered as he burst through the surface, his senses spiralling. To his surprise, he found himself on the far side of the flooded waterway, mere feet from the barn. He could see his teammates scanning the water for him, oblivious to the fact he had surfaced some distance away. He swung wildly, searching for the ghostly bowmen, but they, too, had vanished. What the fuck? Had they ever really been there, or were they just illusions, conjured to distract and delay? The arrow in Brewer said otherwise.

He raised his hands in the air, waving them frantically.

"Oi, over here!" he shouted, lunging forward into a front crawl. O'Hagan was the first to spot him.

"Come on, Fergie, move yer arse and get in; you ain't got time for fucking about!" The others sensed something was amiss and began to add their own desperate words of encouragement. The ghostly bowmen had unnerved them all. It was Brewer this time who managed to voice a warning. Vomit floated next to him on the water, his forehead shone with sweat, but the fast-moving wake appeared right in his line of sight, from their left. Too late for the swimming Marine to hear, let alone act upon.

Fergie had gained little ground when the water began to swell violently around him. The water seemed to part then, and the foul creature rose up from the deep once more, its hulking body blocking his path to safety.

Fergie managed to propel himself backwards with his arms, his feet kicking out, as the beast let out an ungodly roar. Then, with surprising speed, it slammed a monstrous fist down in front of him, sending a funnel of water into the sky and a three-foot wave over his head. He could do little but hold his breath as the momentum propelled his ravaged body back against the bank and he let out a growl of pain. He was on the verge of losing consciousness,but somehow managed to cling on to the bank as the creature advanced. He couldn't pull himself out though. He was done. Exhausted. Ready to give in to the inevitable. All he could do now was look death in the face.

Downs brought his gun up and let off a quick burst into the creature's back. "'Ave some of this!" he growled, but it didn't even flinch. The heavy munition had no effect on its toughened hide. He let off another burst, joined now by O'Hagan eager to bring the abomination down. All it did was annoy it. The creature turned an eyed them, but it didn't return. The message was clear. I'll be back for you after. Downs lowered his weapon.

"Bollocks! What the hell do we do?" The others had no answers and could only stare in helpless silence.

Fergie, meanwhile, had heard the shots. They called him back to himself and, from the recesses of his mind, he heard a familiar voice. The same voice that had, many years ago, urged him to keep going when training, that had ordered him to push through the barrier, to ignore the pain.

That had kept him alive during many a firefight on his deployments. He felt a surge of adrenaline. This was not his time to die. Not here, not like this, and certainly not at the hands of some fucking demon.

He swallowed hard and dragged himself onto the bank, limbs burning from the exertion. In front of him was the barn—and he remembered the tools, makeshift weapons at a pinch. Granted, it wasn't much of a plan, but what the hell, it was worth a punt. His team's intervention had bought him a vital few seconds, which he wasn't going to squander.

He got to his feet and ran along the bank. The creature hissed, keeping pace, stomping relentlessly through the water. It lashed out again, but Fergie saw it coming. He skidded and dropped to his knees as a clenched fist hurtled above and smashed through the wall of the barn. Back on his feet, he motored past the rusted fuel bowser, rounded the corner of the barn, and ran through the open doorway. The sturdy building shook under the thunderous impact as the beast struck again. From above, there came a cracking sound and the front part of the substructure gave way, the heavy timber collapsing on top of the horror outside. It let out a fearsome growl, then began to sweep aside the debris, desperate to continue its hunt.

Fergie found himself screaming, "Just bloody die, will ya!" His head was spinning, his vision blurred. Then he caught sight of the heavy sledgehammer at the far end, resting against a makeshift workbench. He sprinted towards it, the creature close behind, flinging debris left and right. Fergie reached out, grasped the heavy hammer, and spun on his heels, swinging the tool in a wide arc, with a bellow of rage and pain. The foul thing was knocked back on its haunches, a hole punched into its skull. It sat there dumbly for a moment, as though trying to come to terms with a strange new concept. Fergie wasted no time, bracing his foot on its chest to tugged the hammer free. The beast let out a roar of agony as, with a defiant grunt, the Lance Corporal slammed it home for a second time. It tried to back away, but there was just no room.

"Get ta fuck!" rasped Fergie as he swung again, But this time, the creature managed to lash out, the back of its great hand slamming into Fergie's chest. The impact took him clear off his feet and sent him flying across the room, crashing into the workbench.

Through bloodied eyes, he could see his aggressor, up once more and shaking its head like an angry bull. The hammer had slipped from his fingers as he took that last blow. He could see it there now, out of range. Fuck! He slumped onto his side and began to drag himself towards the waterwheel and a small gap, leading to what he presumed were the inner workings. The beast lowered its head, snarling, and stalked towards him, black blood foaming from its nostrils. It bellowed with rage as Fergie neared the hole, grasping his plan of escape, and it charged.

Fergie pulled his legs through and found himself on a narrow wooden ledge. Beneath him, the man-made runoff churned amidst the debris and fast-flowing water, blackened by peat. Ahead of him he could see an opening, a small hatch left ajar. It appeared to be his only chance of escape. He raised up on his elbows and scrambled along while the hellish creature smashed at the wheel and its housing, unable to reach him but willing to bring down the building trying.

Fergie reached the hatch in a matter of seconds, and managed to force it open. He dove through headfirst, landing with a bone-jarring crunch, landing on the riverbank once more.

He had barely regained his feet when the side of the barn shattered behind him, devastated by the berserk rage of the beast. It shouldered its way through the gap, roaring its hate, eyes fixed once more on the Marine. Fergie ran – what else could he do – boots slipping and sliding on the sodden ground.

"Keep going, I've got an idea!" yelled Downs. "A really bad one!" O'Hagan gunned the throttle, the sudden acceleration causing the bow to rise sharply out of the water. Downs slammed in a fresh mag and fired off a round just to get Fergie's attention. When he had it, he gestured over at the trees just past the barn. The Scotsman gave the thumbs-up and, weaving and skidding, headed towards it.

Downs pulled the rifle up and took aim.

"Ain't we already tried shooting this fucker?" snapped O'Hagan. Downs ignored him and drew bead on his target.

"Easy...easy, not yet..." he whispered as Fergie cleared the barn's entrance and the fuel tank next to it.

"Adios, motherfucker" Downs growled as his bullets ripped through the half-filled storage container. With a deafening roar and a blinding flash, the tank exploded, engulfing the creature and the barn alike. Fergie was knocked from his feet by the blast. Downs whooped as the fireball blossomed up and out into the night sky.

"Ho-ly shit," mouthed the Irishman. Downs grinned.

"Told ya it was a bad idea. Now, let's go find the gaffer."

CHAPTER FIFTEEN

Libby heard the bang and looked up, mesmerised by the vast orange mushroom painting the sky up near the church. This wasn't like the sickly glow of town. It was bright and fierce like a firework or a bonfire. She glanced behind her, towards Glastonbury, thinking to compare them. The rain and the wind whipped angrily at her face. She had wondered about making her way there, because there would be a lot more people able to help, but it was just too far. Not to mention the fact that those creatures were still out there somewhere. The further the distance, the more chance she would encounter them, and she shuddered at the thought of that!

She hoped whoever was up at the church would be nice, and would help her find mum and Titan. Her mum had always said that, despite what others say, people are inherently good, and we must always try to see the best in everybody. In fact, that was one of the main reasons her mum had insisted they move to the area. According to her, your vibe attracted your tribe, so what better place to live than Glastonbury, the spiritual capital of Europe? Of course, most people only think of the big music festival when they mention the small market town, but it was the land that made the place special. Or that's what her mum always used to say. One only need open their mind and listen.

Libby used to enjoy their summer day trips into town, the smiling strangers with their long hair and beards, juggling brightly coloured balls; the gnarly old buskers playing pagan folk songs on ancient-looking instruments. If she closed her eyes, she could recall the smell of the fresh fruit and vegetables as they meandered through the market, hand in hand, and feel the jostle of the crowd.

There was always something to see or join in with. Such was the magic of Glastonbury.

Libby wiped the rain from her face as the fireball slowly dissipated, then continued on her way, excited to meet her would-be knights in shining armour.

It was then she heard the definitive rustle of movement. The sound of branches breaking underfoot. The kind of sound that only something big and heavy could make. She froze, shaking in fear, crouching down to be small. She listened intently, but the rain and wind were playing merry hell. Yet nothing attacked. Cautiously, looking about her, she began to move again, step by tiny step. Again came the sound of snapping wood and the brushing of vegetation. She scrunched her eyes tighter against the rain, in a bid to enhance her vision. Nothing to be seen but the bushes. Whatever was stalking her kept just out of reach, concealed in the darkness.

Libby slipped her rucksack off her shoulder. Using only her sense of touch, she tugged it open and dipped her hand inside. Not for a second did she break her vigil, eyes darting all around. She clasped hold of the cold metal handle and pulled the knife free. Her magic sword. She slipped the bag back on then, with trembling hands, she held her weapon out in front of her, daring he stalker to attack. A low growl sounded in the darkness and the girl started to cry, softly, swiping the knife left and right. She couldn't possibly hear breathing out there above the storm, but she sensed it. And she was sure it wasn't human. Libby contemplated stepping backwards, turning, running back towards her home, but she knew it would do her no good. What a stupid girl, coming out here. What did she think she was going to achieve?

She wiped her tears, her breath hitching, and watched in terror as the branches in front of her parted.

CHAPTER SIXTEEN

The young girl wasn't the only one taking an interest in the fiery glow which illuminated the storm-tossed skies.

Two men in black tactical gear paused, dropped to their knees, and silently assessed the surrounding area, one facing in the direction of travel, the other to the rear. Their GEN2 night-vision goggles gave a full and clear image of their bleak surroundings, marred briefly by the distant explosion.

After a couple of minutes, the leader turned, and, using the blade of his hand, signalled forward. Together they rose and began to move once more, their weapons at their shoulders, ready. They knew full well that other things were on the hunt this night, things composed of tooth and claw, fuelled by hate and hunger.

They had infiltrated the area covertly using small, portable jet skis—stowed and concealed now they were near the last known position of the Marine Reserves; from there, it hadn't taken long to locate their targets. They had stayed back to scrutinize and gather intelligence, as per instructions. Still alive. They were almost impressed. Of course, it was imperative to relay said information in real time, and their sophisticated comms equipment had thus far proved reliable. Another team would come in and conduct a clean-sweep operation if the order came down. Such things weren't within their remit. They were eyes on the ground; strictly here to observe and report.

They had been briefed on the incursion taking place in Somerset Levels and, in truth, they weren't fazed at all. They'd seen far worse in their six years of service and had never faced anything that truly felt a threat. They were professionals, after all.

They paused again, near to the flooded river. They looked on in silence as three men in a small inflatable dragged a fourth aboard. They heard muted conversation, laughter, the staccato patter of fear-tinged humour, then, as the Marine Reserves revved away, the Specialist Close Reconnaissance Team watched the building collapse, billowing great plumes of choking black smoke into the sky.

They remained stationary, unwilling to be rushed. They would give it a few more minutes then follow at a safe distance, the oppressive darkness covering their movement. The first man reached to his throat radio, keyed the mic, and awaited a response.

Despite the torrential downpour, they heard a low and guttural growl behind them. The leader managed a half-turn, finger half-pulling the trigger, but that was as far as he got. A viciously-clawed hand swiped down, ripping his head from his shoulders. In the face of such speed and brutality, the second man froze, unable even to raise his weapon.

As the creature began to feast, there was a sharp hiss of static and the radio burst into life.

"Bravo One calling Romeo One. SITREP. Over."

"Romeo One. Come in. Over."

The creature extended a finger and prodded the corpses.

"Romeo One. Do you read? Over."

The abomination grunted and tore off an arm, stripping the flesh with its teeth.

CHAPTER SEVENTEEN

"For fuck's sake, are you mental, or what?" Fergie spluttered, as O'Hagan dragged him into the boat. Downs grinned and patted him on the shoulder. He sucked in a deep breath of air and collapsed between them.

"Yeah, um, sorry about that, Guv. It was a spur-of-the-moment kind of deal. But look on the bright side, at least you're still breathing."

"Only just," said O'Hagan.

"Didn't see *you* coming up with a viable plan," Downs snapped. "Thought you were supposed to be a man of action—the 'Irish Terminator'?"

"Funny. I prefer the term 'Celtic Assassin' meself."

The Scotsman cleared his airway and pulled himself up, perching on one of the seats. He rubbed his forehead and took in the wreckage of the barn, the remnants still ablaze back there in the distance.

"Well, Downs, credit where credit's due," Fergie croaked. Looks like I owe you one."

"Don't mention it, guv. I always wanted to see if it would happen like in the movies."

"Aye? Well, I reckon it worked just fine," said Fergie. "Just...next time, make sure I'm out of the line of fire, eh? I don't fancy getting roasted by one of your half-baked science experiments."

"Hey, boss. I'm glad you're still alive and all, but I reckon we should get a motor on. Pretty sure I just clocked some movement by the treeline," said O'Hagan, grimly.

Fergie turned his attention to Brewer, who sat hunched, clutching his wounded shoulder.

"How ya doing, Captain Egghead? Still with us?"

"I'm not bad, considering," he replied, though he didn't sound convincing.

The Lance Corporal nodded and sucked his teeth. It looked pretty nasty to his eyes. "Aye? Well keep some pressure on the wound for now. Don't try and remove the arrow; you'll only bleed more. As soon as we find shelter, we'll give it the once-over. See what we can do."

He turned to O'Hagan.

"Right then, ya wee bastard. You said it; let's get a move on."

The Irishman didn't need any further prompting. The four Marines braced themselves as the bow rose out of the water, accelerating forward. Brewer slumped back against the shallow wall of the boat, his head lolling to one side. He closed his eyes, grateful for the rest, willing the whole nightmare to be washed away by the stinging December wind.

Fergie took one final look at the burning barn. He would never admit it to anyone, but he'd been mortally afraid back there. Only so many times can a man dodge a bullet. If it hadn't been for Downs' quick thinking, he would have been stone-cold dead. Like Smudger. Christ. All that blood. His crushed body. His soulless eyes staring down at him. Fergie thought of Smudger's daughter, then—Stacy—alone, in tears, never able to see her dad again.

He inhaled nervously and shook his head. This was neither the time nor the place. He stared myopically at the bank and thought that he too caught some fleeting glimpse of movement; ominous shapes amidst the undergrowth, growing in number. A contingent of yellow eyes watching them as they departed. Or was his mind playing tricks?

"Don't worry, boss—I see 'em," Downs whispered, as if reading his mind. He looked about the storm-ravaged boat and caught sight of the familiar shape of the SAW. Good. That'd do. His rifle had been lost to the deluge. He hefted the weapon and detached the magazine. He tapped it on the stock, checked the bullets were seated, then slammed it home. He cocked it and rested the barrel on the side of the boat.

"Obtaining sight picture!" he yelled as he gently squeezed the trigger.

A deafening crack.

A blinding flash.

A quick two-second burst in the direction of their silent observers. Fergie smiled, pleased with the gun's performance, and rested his finger on the trigger guard. He squinted in the spray, maintaining line of sight. Brewer tugged at the Lance Corporal's jacket. Fergie turned to face him.

"What's up?"

"Not to be critical, but what's the plan? We appear to heading for Glastonbury but, well, shouldn't we be getting out of the area? You know, to fetch reinforcements or whatnot. Maybe some of your military chums wouldn't mind lending a hand."

"Mr Brewer, you are not a stupid bloke and I'm pretty sure you've been keeping up with current events. Our arses have been kicked left right and centre."

Brewer remained silent, unnerved by the Marine's suddenly aggressive tone.

"By my reckoning, we wouldn't stand a chance out there in open ground," he added, gesturing into the darkness. "Better to follow the river. Get away from them bastards, find some firmer ground. They might have working comms in town, too."

The young man tried again, reaching for the nub of his concerns. "But...aren't you worried you might lead these things into town? There are thousands of innocent people there.""

There are. Much better odds, wouldn't you say? Might be able to get you some real medical attention while we're at it too—unless you have a better plan?"

Brewer huffed under his breath and slumped back awkwardly. He turned to face the grinning Downs, who had overheard the entire exchange.

"What's so funny?"

"Ah, nothing. I'm just looking forward to seeing the looks on the hippies' faces when we rock up with all this firepower. All the love and light in the world won't help 'em against what's out there."

"Amen to that, brother," quipped O'Hagan.

Brewer shook his head in disgust and returned his attention to the younger Marine.

"How very profound. But that's a bit of a sweeping statement, don't you think, and rather missing the point? They aren't all dope-smoking hippies, you know. There are good people out there. Intelligent people. People who are far more enlightened than you or I. Have you ever been to Glastonbury, Mr Downs?"

"Yeah, only once, back in my student days," said Downs, "but it was a few years ago. Me and some mates jumped the fence at the festival. We got proper off our nuts. In fact, we ended up in a scrap with a bunch of new-agers in one of the local pubs. Ended up spending a night in the cells. Even the coppers were as soft as shit. Try that anywhere else, you'd get a slap from the old bill and sent packing. There's a reason all hell was let loose out here. Easy fucking pickings."

"Granted, circumstances are dire. However, regardless

of the situation, violence is not the only answer. Only those of weak character think in such a way, Mr Downs," Brewer replied.

"Are you for real? Aren't you the one who used a chair leg on the gaffer, or do you have a short memory? Listen, I've got two step-kids and a missus that depend on me, and I'm telling you now that the world is a bad place full of bad people. You may think I'm some kind of uneducated thug, but I can assure you nothing could be further from the truth. I have degrees in both sociology and law. But more importantly, I'm a realist, willing to do what it takes to protect those I love. So, tell you what, Mr Holier-than-thou, you and the space cadets give peace a chance, and me and my 'violent' mates will cover you just in case it doesn't work out, eh? You can thank us after."

O'Hagan let out a soft chuckle. Brewer could feel his temper rising but decided to remain quiet. Such men were a necessary evil, unfortunately. Without them, his chances of survival would be significantly reduced.

And on the plus side, once they reached the relative safety of the town, he should be able to make good his escape. By his reckoning, he could be rid of them in as little as twenty minutes. With his good hand, he reached under his sodden jumper and retrieved the small bundle of fabric containing the spear. He gripped it tightly, warmed by its proximity. These fools, with all their alpha male bluster and their modern weapons. They were only postponing the inevitable. He pulled the wrapped spear close. This was the only real chance of truly defeating the Huldra and escaping the Wild Hunt, and he sure as hell wasn't going to leave it with this bunch of amateurs. No, this was his winning hand. They could do what they liked; when the time was right, he'd take his chance. They'd be nothing more than bait.

O'Hagan's sudden call snapped him back from his musings. Brewer looked up to see the Irishman pointing ahead of them.

"Keep your heads down, folks. Low bridge coming up.

It's gonna be pretty tight." All four occupants strained their eyes to focus on the dark mass bearing down on them.

The underside of the bridge was a mere foot from the waterline. Its thick concrete supports straddled the heavily flooded waterway. They would need to be lying virtually flat in order to pass safely beneath it. An irrational sense of fear surged through his body. Claustrophobia.

The men dropped to their backs, uncomfortable, their bodies pressed against the hard plastic. O'Hagan was the last to move, his hand easing off the throttle. The steady drone of the outboard was almost hypnotic. All else remained silent as the bow edged beneath the shadow of the structure, the darkness stifling. Coffin-like. O'Hagan kept up the pressure as the boat slowly skimmed the surface, its occupants' heads mere inches from the cold stone underside of the bridge, the air pungent with decomposing vegetation Brewer closed his eyes, focusing on the sound of the engine, breathing as slowly as he could without gagging.. Fergie kept peeking forward, alert to any threat, though the lack of headroom made things very difficult. The reassuring frame of the SAW was tucked tight against his body, his finger resting on the trigger guard. He wouldn't like to think what the echo of it's lead would do to their ears in this confined space, but life beat death any day.

In the end, it took them less than twenty seconds to clear the bridge, but to the battle-weary group, it felt more like twenty minutes. Their bodies ached from the cramped positions they'd been jammed in, not to mention the unshakeable sense of dread. Brewer was the first to rise. He stretched his spine, his neck cracking loudly.

"Well, that's a relief. I hate confined spaces. Wasn't sure I would make it."

The speed and the ferocity of the next attack was devastating. The Marines cried out in horror as a skeletal pair of hands appeared from above them and clamped around Brewer's head, its nails digging deep into the meat of his neck. The stunned men looked up into the glinting green eyes of the Huldra.

The deathless creature twisted savagely. As his head came off, his body convulsed violently, the air made foul by his sudden bowel movement. Without thinking, Fergie lunged forward and grabbed hold of Brewer's legs, as though to save him somehow. He was rewarded by nothing more than a hot torrent of blood and a foul stench of shit as the torso hit the floor. O'Hagan ducked down, fearful of a second attack, and gunned the throttle. The other two men were thrown off balance, the sudden and uncontrolled acceleration nearly lifting the boat from the water and bouncing them off the bank. The Irishman snatched the tiller, causing the boat's port side to drop violently.

"Hold on!" bellowed O'Hagan as the boat rocked violently from side-to-side. Downs let off a wild burst, his bullets smashing into worn concrete. Meanwhile, Fergie hefted the SAW, ready to pump some serious lead. He was about to squeeze the triggerwhen another jarring movement forced the boat starboard, throwing off his aim. If he hadn't been leaning that way the Scot might have gone overboard. He shot O'Hagan a glare.

"What the hell are you playing at, laddie? Ease up! Yer gonna kill us!"

"Really? Take a look, lads!" screamed the Irishman.

Downs and Fergie held their breath, as along the banks more creatures appeared.

"Oh Jesus," mouthed Downs, as the demons began to keep pace, some upright, others galloping on all fours. Fergie swung the SAW up to eye-level and let them have it, volley after volley.. He felt no relief as each fallen fucker was seemingly replenished by four more.The horde appeared similar in make up to their initial encounter, a gathering of the truly macabre. Ectomorphic creatures with wicked-looking talons, their limbs muscular yet strangely at odds with their size. Behemoth trolls, their features grotesque and gnarled, and apparitions of warriors, long-dead.

The boat hit a sudden swell and leapt from the water. All three of the surviving men snatched at the grab handles as it crashed back down, the impact sending a surge of water across the deck. Brewer's body rolled and flopped, getting half-wedged beneath the seat. O'Hagan cursed and struggled to bring the speeding boat under control once more, whilst Fergie continued firing while Downs reloaded, each struggling to keep their balance.

With the boat settling once more, Downs opened fired, cursing as he missed his target yet again. This time the closest creature lunged from the bank, its claws extended. Downs turned, trying to dodge the incoming attack but he slipped and crashed to the floor, his head slamming into the thick rubber seat. As he did so, his finger squeezed, letting off four rounds before the bolt snapped back. Above him, the monstrosity hissed as three of the projectiles found their mark, punching through the soft tissue of its belly and exiting through its back. In the blur of the moment, Fergie caught the briefest of glimpses as the thing tumbled between himself and Downs and landed in the water behind them with a splash.

"Where the hell did it go?" Fergie snarled as he swung the heavy weapon in a wide arc.

Downs dragged himself to his knees, his head ringing from the impact.

"I lost sight of it. Not sure if I actually hit anything," he replied, shakily. Both men kept their weapons up, each sweeping the gloom.

O'Hagan pushed harder, the boat building speed now he was holding her steady, but the outboard was screaming. It did not sound happy. The Irishman was breathing heavily, his vision blurred and stinging from the spray. He wiped his face and said a silent prayer to any merciful deity who might be nearby.

"Fuck!" screamed Downs, as they rounded a corner.

"It's blocked! What's that, flood defences? Fuck's sake."

"We've got no choice but to dump the boat. Get ready, boys!" Fergie strained through the darkness. Downs reloaded.

"Last mag!" he bellowed, and he opened fire. The creatures sensed the chase was almost at an end and bounded forward with razor-sharp grins,heading for the barricade.

"What the hell do we do now?" barked Downs between rounds. Head back?

"How wide do they make those things?" shouted Fergie.

"Flood defences? How the fuck would I know?" snapped O'Hagan. "Ten, fifteen feet, maybe. Big enough to be a problem."

"What's the chances of having another usable waterway on the far side?"

O'Hagan shrugged.

"Fifty-fifty, I reckon."

"It's flooded, right? So, there should be surface water on top, at least a few inches, right? Enough for us to skim the top and carry us over. Like tossing pebbles. Whaddya say?

"Bloody hell, mate, that's insane! We're a damn sight heavier than a pebble. We'd have to drop some weight to even contemplate it."

Fergie lay down the machine gun and grabbed hold of Brewer's remains. He had to tug to get him un-wedged and, as he did so, the little bundle of rags fell clear. He stamped on it with his foot, holding it in place then, with an explosive surge of strength, Fergie tossed the corpse overboard.

"Let's do it," he snapped, retrieving the artefact and tucking it in his jacket.

We're still gonna have to hit it at some speed to get across there. I can circle around, give us a run up. But what about those...?"

The cluster of creatures were gathering now upon the flood defence, cackling and sniping.

"Fuck it! Go through 'em," rasped Fergie.

O'Hagan manoeuvred the boat, got it lined up just as he'd said, and then he paused, revving the engine. "Are you sure about this, boys? We really doing this?

"We've gotta do something," Downs said, with bravado. "This shit's getting really fucking old."

"Aye. Gun it."

The Irishman grimaced and maxed out the throttle.

"Oh well, at least we'll go out in style," he croaked.

CHAPTER EIGHTEEN

The Augusta Westland 109 Power Grand helicopter lurched violently, causing Sir Malcolm Hawker to snatch hold of the leather safety handle. He steadied himself and sucked in a nervous lungful of air.

"Sorry about that, Sir Malcolm," came a soothing voice over his headphones. "We hit a small pocket of turbulence. All being well, it should be plain sailing from hereon in." There was a short hiss of static.

Hawker pressed the small switch in his armrest.

"No need to apologise, Captain. I'm sure I'm in safe hands. Out of curiosity, what is our ETA for landing?"

Another hiss of static.

"Current flight time to Bristol is just under fifteen minutes. At this moment in time, the weather seems to be holding and it should be clear for us to land. However, the storm surge is unpredictable and could turn nasty. Rest assured, we will keep you informed of any developments, sir."

"Thank you," he replied, reaching for his whiskey tumbler.

He sat back and stared out of the window, pitch-black save for occasional specks of fluorescent light below them, blurred by rain. He had little time for flying death traps, but they were a necessary evil, especially when time was of the essence.

He had digested the latest intelligence report regarding the ongoing Somerset situation, and was now evaluating his options. According to the briefing, the small group of

Royal Marine Reservists were proving to be a little too resilient, despite being severely out of their depth. Some people within the organisation had wondered whether they should be impressed by their tenacity or concerned that they might be a security risk. As far as Hawker was concerned, it was a false binary. In his line of work, not to mention his position, it was paramount to remain objective —regardless of personal feelings, one must always err on the side of caution.

He took a hefty swig and replaced the heavy glass on the small table in front of him. He picked up the thick manilla file containing the military records of those involved, and flipped it open. As expected, they were a ragtag mix of the lower class, salt-of-the-earth types with a catalogue of broken homes, patchwork parenting, and menial jobs. All of them clearly lacked the gall or the lineage to attain any decent rank within Her Majesty's Armed Forces. The only one with any semblance of education had two unimpressive degrees from an establishment of dubious quality. Anybody could obtain such 'qualifications' these days. Occasionally, in isolated moments of weakness, he felt sorry for those born without such privileges, but anyone of true character would rise without them.

The sudden hiss of static filled his earphones, followed by the relaxed and confident voice of the captain.

"Just to let you know, sir, we have made better headway than expected. It appears the storm has abated sufficiently, and has yet to change course. We are beginning our descent now and should be on the ground within five minutes."

Hawker smiled and settled back in his seat.

"Excellent news, Captain. I trust you will do me the service of alerting my associates on the ground? Please have them waiting once we land."

"Of course, sir. I have already made the arrangements."

"A sterling job as ever, Captain."

Hawker felt the helicopter drop slightly then bank to starboard. He looked out of the window at the bright lights of Bristol Airport below, glanced at his watch, then straightened his shirt cuffs. His brow was slightly damp, he noted, dabbing at it with a handkerchief. The landing was always the worst part.

The rotor was still winding down as the co-pilot helped Hawker down from the helicopter. He turned up the collar of his jacket, shielding his face from the downdraft, and took in the welcoming party. Three Range Rovers waited for him. A well-dressed man stood at the rear door of the nearest, holding it open for him. Hawker gave him a curt nod. Upon entry, Hawker wasted little time on pleasantries with the occupant sharing the back seat.

"Well?" he asked abruptly. "Situation report, Mr Roberts."

"Nice to see you too, Mr Hawker. The old whirlybird got you a little anxious, has it?"

Hawker glared at his companion. He'd grown used to the man's calculated disrespect, but it still annoyed him. Roberts glared right back, his slate-grey eyes unwavering.

"If God had intended us to fly, he would have given us wings, Mr Roberts."

Roberts smiled. Baiting the bigwigs was one of his favourite pastimes.

Roberts was a bear of a man. Six-foot-six of well-chiselled muscle, cropped hair, and a freshly-shaven face. Ex-military, of course. He made his living from violence—by all accounts, very successfully. Most people would, if they were smart, steer well clear of the man. If they lacked intelligence, well, they'd soon learn their lesson. Hawker disliked the man and felt no need to disguise the fact. In truth, he hadn't been employed for his sparkling personality; he was the organisation's hammer, a blunt-force weapon to be unleashed when all other options had been exhausted.

"I thought you and your team were supposed to be landing at Yeovilton, Mr Roberts. Why the sudden diversion? Everything is on schedule, I trust?"

Roberts huffed. He hated explaining himself, particularly to posh knobs like Hawker.

"Way too much activity at that particular base. The emergency services are coordinating with military assets. It's over-run with police, fire service and the like. Easier to blend into the background here. Nice private landing area, far from the public's prying eyes. Don't panic, nothing's changed, and yes, everything is on schedule. It's an hour's drive to the RV, and my men have been fully briefed. It's what you pay me for."

Hawker smiled and glanced up at the two men dressed in black sitting quietly in the front seats.

"Glad to hear it. Now, how experienced is your team? There's room for trainees on this mission, I'm sure you understand."

Hawker was pleased to note Roberts' temples were throbbing, but he managed to keep his smile inside.

"They are all former boy scouts; what the hell do you take me for?"

"No need to get defensive, Mr Roberts. Just humour me please, and answer the question."

Roberts sucked in a breath, struggling to keep his composure.

"Tier One, ten-man team. All former SPEC-OP. Experienced in our particular working environment and fully aware of the mission parameters. Satisfied?"

"And we are carrying the full range of ordinance, should it be deemed necessary?" Roberts added, to drive his point home.

Hawker coughed quietly into his handkerchief and returned it to his jacket pocket. "Forgive me, Mr Roberts. I do not for a second doubt your abilities, but this isn't just some low-level incursion. Indeed, it has escalated seriously over the last hour. Add to that a group of armed men who need to be dealt with, men with similar backgrounds as yourself—I trust that won't be an issue?"

The big man gently touched the sub-machine gun resting on his lap.

"Don't worry, old-timer. You tend to your business, and we'll tend to ours."

Hawker felt his jaw muscles clench at the jibe, but he nodded.

"Well then. So long as we are clear. Let's get to it, then." And he leaned back into the soft leather seat.

Roberts nodded and tapped the driver on the shoulder. They pulled away, the other two vehicles following behind.

CHAPTER NINETEEN

The sound of the boat hitting the blockade was a piercing shriek, as the boat skidded across the structure with a bone-jarring crash, straight through the nightmare mob of creatures. There was a chorus of wails and screams as the bow burst through, battering their bodies aside or crushing them beneath. Fergie snapped the machine gun to eye-level, picking his shots. This thing was wider than he expected, and and the floodwater here was barely deep enough for the propeller to have an effect. Fergie felt a sudden surge of panic as he felt the boat slowing.

"Keep going, keep going!" he roared, and O'Hagan gave it more revs. Downs checked his magazine and slammed it back into the receiver.

"Ten rounds left, boss!" he yelled, as one of the creatures charged towards him. It was no more than two feet away when he pumped a three-round burst into its head, dropping it instantly.

O'Hagan kept up the pace and held his breath as the hard rubber of the underside scraped the concrete hidden beneath. Smoke started to rise from the outboard. He couldn't bring himself to take in his surroundings; his peripheral vision was enough. More beasts closing in, the unseen pendulum of battle swinging in their pursuer's favour. His stomach tightened, then flipped in fear and relief as the boat dropped down the other side with a great splash, finding deeper water once more. He worked the tiller hard, the boat zigzagging across the water, the outboard given new purchase and catching him off-guard.

Fergie and Downs could do little but hold on. Fergie looked back at the creatures who finally began to fall behind, their shrills of pain and rage diminishing.

"How ya doing, fella?" Fergie asked Downs as they slumped back once more, his voice tinged with concern.

Downs flashed a half-grin, yet his eyes and his breathing told another story. He returned to his rifle scope without so much as a word. Yeah. He was fucked. They all were. What was the point in talking about it? Afterwards, maybe. Right now, they just had to get through it.

The silence stagnated for a while as they made their way upriver, buffeted by the wind, spat at by the rain and spray, each man lost in his own thoughts of grief, fear and regret. It was O'Hagan who broke in the end, pinning their problem down.

"What's the actual plan, boss? Coz I'm starting to think there's only one way this is gonna end, and it ain't good!" Fergie turned to face the Irishman, unable to stop his limbs from shaking in the cold night air. He balled his fists and caught his breath, hating to show any weakness. Out there, on the horizon was a cluster of lights, like jewels in the darkness.

"That's got to be Glastonbury," he said. "The electric's on, so that give us hope. Comms. Supplies. Back-up. Medical. We'll on the water for as long as possible, then ditch the boat and yomp the rest of the way."

The Irishman remained silent, but Fergie could sense his trepidation.

"What's up? If you've got something to say, spit it out, man. We've got no time to piss about second-guessing each other."

"Well, it's just... What the hell are we going do when we get there? Brewer was right about one thing: those hippies aren't exactly gonna be up for the fight. Even if we manage to raise the Army, they won't be able to get out here quickly, and we've only got a handful of rounds left. What are we gonna use if those things catch up with us?"

"He may be a wanker, but he's got a point, Fergie,"

Downs mumbled.

Fergie slumped onto one of the seats, its surface still sopping with Brewer's blood. He reached under his jacket and produced the spear bundle.

"Well, our boffin was clinging on to this thing like grim death. Seemed to reckon that it was the only way to properly finish that hell-bitch off. So the way I see it, we have only got one chance to get out of this alive, we've got to lure her in. Get in close and stick this spear right down her fucking throat!"

It was then that Downs noticed something moving on the bank, approximately fifty yards ahead of their position. He stood up quickly, and the sudden movement set the boat rocking. Weapons hit hands. He swung up his rifle.

"There. On the bank, eleven o'clock. Two figures," he growled.

O'Hagan and Fergie edged forward, tightly wound, looking for the threat, ready to open fire. The figures remained motionless, unthreatening, and strangely silent. It was only as they drew up close perspective sharpening, that they realised what they were seeing.

"Can this shit get any fucking weirder?" said Fergie, as the young girl began waving at them, a radiant smile breaking through the filth on her face. As if the sight of this child out here amidst the carnage wasn't strange enough, the imposing mass of her German Shepherd—the largest the Scotsman had ever seen, standing guard over her—rendered him speechless.

CHAPTER TWENTY

The men stared at the young girl, with increasing wonder as she recounted her tale. Downs was visibly moved as her voice broke when mentioning her missing mother, his mind no doubt flying to his own step-children—yet she became excited and joyful when relaying the moment she was reunited with her dog. Such was the resilience of youth. Fergie kept his voice as low and as even as possible so as not to agitate the girl or her shaggy guardian. He cleared his throat and leaned forward, the moored boat rising and falling on the water.

"Wow, what can I say? That's—um—that's a pretty wild adventure you've been on. Got to say I'm impressed..."

He paused, realising she hadn't told them her name.

"Libby. My name is Libby Hooper, and this," she said, patting her companion on the head, "is Titan."

Fergie shook her hand.

"Nice to meet you, Libby Hooper. And you too, Titan. Good name for a mighty beast." He straightened himself up and addressed her more formally.

"My name is Lance Corporal Ferguson, but you can call me Fergie. And these two reprobates," he said, grinning "are Downs and O'Hagan."

"We are Royal Marines," said Downs. "Do you know what that is?"

"I sure do," Libby replied quickly. "My dad was in the Army. He said Royal Marines were security guards for the Navy, and that the Paras were the *real* soldiers."

"Jesus. Even the kids have got it in for us tonight," said O'Hagan, pretending to be hurt.

They couldn't help but chuckle at her unintentional jibe.

"Hey, Libby, could I get off the boat and come ashore? I promise we're not here to hurt you," said Fergie, as he glanced at her stationary sentinel.

"It's just, I don't fancy becoming Titan's dinner."

The young girl let out an infectious giggle and patted the dog's head.

"It's OK, Titan; Fergie and his friends are here to help us." The dog immediately lay down, his tongue lolloping to one side, evidently content with his mistress' command. Fergie stepped off the boat and onto the sodden bank.

"Where were you heading, anyway, Libby?" he asked softly. "Glastonbury is over that way."

Libby shrugged her shoulders. "Well, after mum left, I heard loud bangs and saw some bright flashes coming from the old church. It was closer to us than Glastonbury, and I knew that there must be people up there. People with the right equipment to help me find my mum. It would be pretty stupid to be out here if they didn't."

Fergie was pleased by the young girl's reasoning, her courage, and her self-control. She was a tough cookie, this one.

"Wow, that's pretty clever, weren't you scared?"

"Sometimes I was scared, but that's when you have to be brave. And look, I found Titan! I just wish I knew where mum is."

"Well, Libby. We're on our way to Glastonbury now. There's too many monsters back that way for you to be safe. I reckon you should come with us. We can send a search party out for your mum once we get there. What d'ya think?"

Libby cocked her head, weighing up her options.

"Can Titan come with us?"

Fergie patted the smiling German Shepherd on the head.

"Well, of course! We wouldn't dream of leaving him out here. Where you go, he goes. Say, Libby—does this waterway go all the way to Glastonbury?"

"No," she said. "It stops just outside the town."

Fergie nodded. "Right, lads, new plan. We take Libby and Titan with us, follow the water until it terminates, then hoof it into town."

"What about weapons, boss?" asked Downs. "If those things show up...." Libby butted in. "My dad used to go clay pigeon shooting. I got to go with him sometimes. We used to stop at the shooting shop on the way so he could buy cartridges."

The Marines looked visibly stunned at this.

"What else do they sell, Libby?" asked Fergie.

"Shotguns, ammunition, rifles, hunting supplies. You know, the usual stuff country people need," she replied jovially.

"Libby—" he said, ruffling her hair. She giggled. "—you really are something special. Whereabouts is this gun shop? Is it this side of town?"

"Yep. It's about a ten-minute walk once we get there. I know the way...."

She paused as if she were concerned about something.

"Um, you do know it's night-time and that it won't be open, right?"

O'Hagan winked at their young ward.

"Don't worry about that, little lady. We have a special key."

Fergie took one last look around as they boarded the boat, then they pushed off from the bank.

"Right, lads, keep yer eyes peeled, stay frosty, and let's get the hell out of here. We're on the homeward stretch now."

O'Hagan gently twisted the throttle, then when on course, opened it up. Libby sat back, clinging on to Titan, who just sat there, ears flapping in the wind, deeply unimpressed by this new mode of transport. She let out a giggle as the spray flew, causing her to scrunch her eyes up tight. The look of joy on her face was infectious, and soon the lot of them were smiling. It seemed they'd found some hope after all.

CHAPTER TWENTY ONE

The fluorescent lights cast puddles of neon across the wet tarmac and abandoned vehicles. With an ear-splitting crash, the door burst in under the force of O'Hagan's heavy boot. He flashed a smile at Libby, whose mouth hung open.

"See? Special key," he quipped. Downs edged past and carefully entered the gun shop. No alarm sounded, much to their surprise.

"Probably tripped a silent one, hooked up to the old bill," said the Marine. "I don't think we've got anything to worry about though. I reckon they've got bigger fish to fry."

O'Hagan made his way through the vandalised door. "You're probably right," he huffed. "It's just a bit weird that we haven't seen anybody. Not one single person. I know it's late, but I was sure there'd be a few still staggering around."

Fergie stayed still, anxiously listening for sirens. *Or would that be a welcoming sound?* All he could hear was the continuous roar of the wind and the rain. *Well, at least this part of town isn't flooded*, he thought. Easier to move around. After one last scan of the area, he followed the others inside.

The interior was in near-total darkness, save for a handful of tiny spotlights illuminating select cabinets. The Scotsman took a minute to acclimatise and assess the stock on display.

"Ooooo-weeee," exclaimed Downs as he walked along a rack of shotguns, tracing the metal and highly-polished wood with his fingers with childlike glee.

"Got us some quality kit in here. Beretta, Benelli,

Mossberg. Even got a few I've never heard of. I reckon we've just hit the jackpot. Spoilt for bloody choice."

Fergie moved purposefully through the shop towards the counter and what he presumed was the ammunition cabinet. It was securely fastened to the substructure of the building, its solid-looking bulk impressive, albeit concerning.

"Right, lads, don't mess about," he said. "Forget all the fancy two-shot shit. Get the high-capacity pumps or semi-autos. We're gonna need as much firepower as we can get. We ain't going clay pigeon shooting and we ain't a bunch of toffs."

Libby stood just inside the doorway, Titan at her heels. She took in her surroundings and watched as her new-found friends inspected their choice of weapons, joshing and murmuring to each other. Downs grinned and hefted a Mossberg tactical ten-shot with pump action. He racked it, the sound echoing within the confines of the empty shop.

"Oh, *hell* yeah! *That's* what I'm talking about!"

Beside him, the equally enthralled O'Hagan worked the charging handle of a Benelli M4 semi-auto. The sharp metallic snap was pleasing to the ear, the weight in his arms comforting.

"Yeah, yeah, Rambo, you can keep yer Mossberg, fella. I'll stick with good old-fashioned Italian reliability any day. If it's good enough for SPEC-OPS, it's good enough for me."

O'Hagan made his way to the row of rifles on the far side of the shop.

"Hey, Downs. Check this out. .308's, .223's, .338 Lapuas. Top-drawer stuff. What d'ya reckon, worth a punt?"

Downs nodded enthusiastically.

"Yeah, get one of those Tikka .308's. It's a mag-fed bolt action. Excellent rifle. Might prove useful if we want to reach out and touch somebody, if you know what I mean. Pop it at the back ready to take with us—we sure as shit can't use it in here. And make sure you get a few extra mags."

O'Hagan nodded, making his way to the rear of the store as he spoke. "Alright. Come on, then. Let's get organized. I'll get some kit together, you go help the gaffer stock up on ammo. Oh! And make sure you get some solid slug; that stuff'll bring down a friggin' elephant!"

Downs turned to Libby. "Congratulations, Marine. You have just enlisted. You stay there, OK? Don't leave the shop but keep a lookout—if you see anybody, give us a shout. "

The youngster saluted and turned to face the door, her canine protector steadfast at her side.

"Goddammit!" hissed Fergie. He pulled open drawer after drawer beneath the counter, looking for the cabinet keys. A sudden noise close behind startled him. He turned, but instead of a friendly face, found himself looking down the business end of a twelve-gauge.

"Who the hell are you?" spat the overweight, elderly man hefting the weapon. Fergie took a step back, his hands aloft.

"Wow! Easy, old-timer. We don't want that thing going off now, do we?"

The man pulled the shotgun deeper into his shoulder and tightened his grip.

"I don't know about that. You boys are burglars, caught red-handed. I reckon the police wouldn't care if I shot you where you stand."

Fergie was impressed with the old-timer's grit.

"I like yer style, fella, but do we really look like criminals? Just take a wee look at our uniforms."

The old man didn't bat an eye.

"Anyone can get one of those online. Now, move a muscle and I'm going to squeeze this trigger. Now, which of you is going to call the police for me?"

He took a step forward, the twin barrels edging closer to the Scotsman's face. Downs and O'Hagan appeared, their weapons raised, unsure how to proceed. It was one thing to shoot a monster, but old men was a different kettle of fish.

"Look, mate, trust me, we really are Royal Marine Reservists. Lance Corporal William Ferguson at your service. These are Marines Downs and O'Hagan. We were on an exercise up on Ham Hill when the storm hit. Our orders were to head down into the outlying villages and assist with civilian EVAQ, but then things got a little... complicated."

The old man scrutinized the Scotsman.

"What do you mean, *complicated*?"

"Seriously? Haven't you noticed anything strange this evening? Nothing out of the ordinary?"

"This is Glastonbury, in case you hadn't noticed. It's *all* bloody strange here."

"Please don't hurt him, Mr Ower. They're my friends."

The men turned to see Libby making her way towards them. The store owner gaped.

Libby's story, as she told it, was hard to believe. Too much imagination, that one. But sweeping aside her fairy-tale details, it tallied well enough with the soldiers' story of a hostile force. Terrorists, maybe. Or do-gooders, like them XR kids raising merry hell. He sucked his teeth and squinted up at Fergie then, with care, he brought his gun down and made it safe.

"I've known Libby and her family for a great number of years. Good people. Honest. If she says you boys are legit, then I find no reason to doubt her. You have her to thank for the fact you boys are still breathing."

"Aye, she's a star that one, and no mistake. I hope we can get her reunited with her mammie. You say you know the family. Can you give their house a call in case the woman's returned? She'd be going out of her mind with worry if she has."

"Indeed. I shall need to to look it up, but we do hold records of all our customers. Legal requirement, you know." He bustled off, followed by Downs who didn't yet trust him to be alone.

***

Fergie stretched his neck and rubbed his eyes. They had managed to secure weapons and ammunition. That was a good start. Next up, he'd need to try to call base. God, he hoped they were reachable. He was dog tired and sick of shouldering all this responsibility. Sick of feeling alone. The shop owner and Downs returned shortly after. They'd had joy getting through to the Hooper household. The phone lines must be down, they figured. High winds and all.

"Listen, young man, far be it for me to tell you how to do your job, but I think the best thing you boys could do is to hunker down here. It's secure, we have supplies, and I can even sort you out a meal and a cup of tea. Or coffee. How's that sound? There's no shame in lying low and waiting for the cavalry, eh? Just a shame you can't call in some heavy air support in this wretched weather."

"Trust me, we've tried," retorted the Scotsman. "I'd settle for bloody EasyJet lobbing suitcases right about now."

Fergie glanced around to see Libby and Downs looking on, eager for him to agree to the offer. Hell, even O'Hagan had paused what he was doing to take note.

"Fine. Well, I mean, yeah, thank you. We appreciate it." There was a muted acknowledgement and a sense of relief from the rest of them.

"Well, better get to barricading the front door and setting up some defences. Remember last time?" said Downs as he made his way to the front of the shop, O'Hagan close behind. Libby moved forward and snaked her arms around the older man, hugging him.

"Thank you, Mr Ower."

The shop owner ruffled the top of her head.

"You are welcome, Libby. I'm going to get the kettle on and sort out some food. Keep an eye on this lot."

Fergie playfully punched the young girl on the arm and grinned.

"Right then, you gonna help us with the defences, or what?"

Libby straightened up and saluted.

"Marine Hooper reporting for duty, sir."

***

It took just under an hour to rig up a makeshift barricade and fortify the building. Whatever force had prevented their comms from working on the Levels still seemed to be in play. Fergie had started to suspect it was something more than bad weather. Downs had done a pretty good job of sealing the broken door. Next, they had managed to drag a couple of the centre display racks in front of the large window. It was reinforced security glass, but Fergie didn't want to take any chances considering what had happened in the church. To top it all off, O'Hagan had strategically placed five or six loaded shotguns along with stashes of ammo around the perimeter of the lower building. Windows and doors had been secured and, where possible, blocked. Meanwhile, Downs had gone upstairs to do much the same. Nothing was a hundred percent, but it was workable.

Of course, they had a contingency plan. Mr Ower took them down into the cellar to show them an unused tunnel. The building had once been a coaching inn, he explained, dating back to the sixteen-hundreds, and this tunnel was supposedly used by Parliamentarians to escape Royalist forces just prior to the battle of Sedgemoor, which was close by. The Marines weren't bothered by the history, they were just seeing its tactical potential—it was perfect for their needs.

O'Hagan had explored the short tunnel, which led to a solid stone outbuilding at the end of the garden, and made sure its exit was both unhampered and undetectable from the outside. Satisfied, he set up rucksacks containing food, water, ammunition, and a few more shotguns to pick up on retreat. Reserves or not, they were Marines. It paid to be prepared.

"Well, what do you think?" asked O'Hagan.

Fergie turned to face the Irishman, who was busy lighting a roll-up. He blew out a steady stream of smoke then offered it to Fergie, who declined.

"About what?"

"About how the hell we're gonna get out of this in one piece. Not to mention how we are gonna explain what happened."

"Havnae got a clue, pal. I'm just winging it at the moment. If we can last the night, then maybe we can get out with our balls intact. As for explaining it, I've not really given it much thought. More pressing things to worry about, know what I mean?"

The Irishman took another drag and gestured across to Libby, who was busily feeding Titan some pasta hoops. He hissed smoke through his teeth and asked the question neither man wanted to face.

"What about her? We both know her mum is dead; no way she could have survived out there against those things.

If you ask me, I say we leave her here with the old man. Never look back." He held up his hands at Fergie's glare. "It's harsh, I know, but come on, Ferg. Whether you like it or not, she'll slow us down."

"Pish! Aye, her mum's probably dead but I'm sure as hell not leaving her behind. The old codger couldn't fight his way out of a paper bag, let alone defend her if them things come tae call. She comes with. Understand?"

O'Hagan held his hands up again. Defeated.

"Just talking out loud, is all, boss man. I'll back your play regardless, you know that."

Fergie knew deep down he was probably half-right. Truth be told, the thought of leaving her had crossed his mind when they'd first arrived. But now, seeing her behaving how a child of her age should, his moral core couldn't justify leaving her to an uncertain fate.

He hefted his shotgun and made his way down to the back of the shop, where Ower and Downs sat quietly drinking mugs of fresh coffee.

"Dinnae suppose there's any going spare?" he asked. Downs nodded, and after pouring a cup, slid it across the counter. Fergie took a sip and winced as the hot liquid burnt his lips. Ower chuckled.

"All this, and you get bested by a mug of coffee, eh?"

"Well, you know, even us Royal Marines get caught out. Sometimes by old-timer's with a shotgun."

"Yes, sorry about that. To be fair, you lot were bloody noisy. Not exactly master criminals."

"Trust me, we dinnae make a habit of breaking and entry."

Ower fussed about preparing a home-made soup for them. Nothing fancy, he said, but he hoped a little sustenance would do them good. He put the heating up for them too and, once the soup began to bubble, he offered them some dry socks. Nothing worse than cold, wet feet, was there? Fergie gave assent, grateful for the man's thoughtfulness.

Downs and Fergie sat there silently, each caught up in thoughts of the dead, fears for the future, and problems that seemed to have no solutions. Fergie pulled out the rag containing Brewer's spearhead and unwrapped it, admiring the fine workmanship. Somehow... Somehow he was going to have to get close enough to use this.

***

Out front, Libby had her face pressed up against the window. Titan was growling softly next to her.

"Fergie, are these your friends out here? Have they come to rescue us?"

The Scotsman got to his feet and moved quickly to her side. Downs and O'Hagan immediately took up flanking positions, weapons up, safeties off. They strained to see through the rain-battered glass but there were no signs of movement.

"What did you see, Libby? I don't see anything."

The young girl pointed across the road.

"I saw people dressed in black, moving behind those cars. They were carrying weapons. I think they were soldiers."

Again, Fergie scanned the darkness but saw nothing. He turned to face his subordinates, neither of whom looked particularly convinced.

"O'Hagan, Downs. Anything?"

Both men shook their heads.

Fergie relaxed and turned to Libby.

Stuart R Brogan

"I think you might have been imagining—"

And then the night was shattered by gunfire.

CHAPTER TWENTY TWO

The sudden attack was deafening. On instinct, Fergie threw himself forward, taking Libby to the floor. The impact punched the air from her lungs and she lay there beneath him, silently wailing her terror and pain. Using his body as a shield, he kept her down as a second wave of bullets ripped through the window, slamming into walls and shelving. She buried her face into his chest, and clung on tight. His ears were ringing from the maelstrom as chaos reigned once more. Around them, the whirlwind of violence continued; the only other sounds were those of Libby's sobbing now she'd regained her breath, and the guttural growl of Titan. Fergie pulled in his extremities, trying to reduce his mass, his body now adorned by a glistening blanket of glass fragments and shards of splintered wood.

"O'Hagan! Downs!" he bellowed, as another burst of rounds poured in. He managed a fleeting glance just in time to see the Irishman on the far side of the room levelling his shotgun and blasting off a three-shot burst. Downs knelt by his side, primed for retaliation. Fergie felt a momentary wave of relief that his men were uninjured, performing just as they'd been trained. His pride turned to horror in moments as O'Hagan took a headshot: a single, just above his right eye, sending a spray of blood and brains across the plasterwork. Fergie watched helplessly as his lifeless body dropped to the floor, twitching, the shotgun sliding from his hands. Downs let out a roar, his face and clothing spattered with gore. He got to his feet, working the pump on his shotgun, and fired five shots in quick succession. They were answered immediately by another punishing volley from their unknown attackers.

Downs slumped to his knees behind cover, gasping, a stream of blood flowing down, gathering in his left eye. He wiped it away with the back of his dirt-encrusted hand, and shot Fergie a question.

"Who the fuck are this lot? It can't be those fairy fuckers, surely!"He began thumbing fresh shells into the Mossberg.

"No fucking clue," rasped Fergie, "but whoever they are, they're packing some serious heat."

"Fergie man, we gotta get the fuck out of here; we got no choice. We can't match that kind of firepower!" Downs racked the pump-action, loading a fresh shell into the chamber.

Libby sat curled on the floor now, cradling her head in her hands. Fergie put his hand to her face.

"Libby, Libby, you OK? Can you hear me?" She opened her eyes and nodded, her grubby face streaked with tears.

"Oh, thank God! I thought you'd been hit or something." He pulled her to his chest.

"Where's Ower?" asked Downs, popping up to let loose three more shots then ducking back down again behind the barricade.

The Scotsman locked eyes with the little girl.

"Listen to me and listen good, girlie. You have to be brave. I'm gonna have to move now. I've got to see if Mr Ower is OK. You understand? Can you be brave for me and stay here, tucked away? Watch over Titan and young Downs until I get back?"

The young girl nodded, and sniffed.

"Yes. I can be brave," she whispered.

"Good girl." Fergie held up three fingers. Downs nodded as the Scotsman counted down. Fergie leapt his feet and sprinted towards the back of the shop. At the same time, Downs cleared the barricade and let off six rounds, the whiff of gunpowder sharp as each of the shells was ejected.

***

Fergie powered through the shop, his body low, the sound of the shotgun's punishing report echoing behind him as he sought Ower amidst the devastation. He spotted the body, half-buried by debris.

The Marine dropped to his knees beside the corpse; the right side of the old man's chest was punctured by three bullet holes.

"Bastards!" growled Fergie through clenched teeth. The gunfire ceased abruptly and a distant, yet powerful voice addressed him.

"Lance Corporal William Ferguson! I know you are in there; I trust you are still alive—at least, I hope so. I think it's time we had a little chat. Don't you? My men will not open fire again until such time as our parley is concluded."

The Scotsman rose to his feet and cautiously made his way back to the barricade. He threw a quick wink at Libby, who gave him the thumbs-up. *Damn, this girl is tough.*

Downs was busy reloading, hands shaking from the adrenaline. "I'm presuming you heard that, eh, boss. Who the hell is this guy?"

"I havnae got a scooby, fella, but I think it's time we found out." said Fergie.

Before Downs could protest, Fergie stood up, arms outstretched to show he was unarmed, and he moved closer to the gaping window. From the darkness, the silhouettes of ten men gradually appeared, each dressed in black tactical gear, weapons trained upon him. Fergie inspected their skirmish line until his eyes settled on the apparent leader.

"Yeah, I'm Ferguson. Who the hell are you?"

The leader strode forward confidently, the rest of his men stayed put. That was a good sign. It meant they were well-disciplined. Unlikely to engage unless so-commanded.

The leader was tall, well-built, and he had a way about him—posture perhaps, an arrogant calm—that smacked of Special Ops. He approached the shattered window and paused, trying to instil a sense of psychological dominance.

As it happened, Fergie was doing the same. He may not have gone to some flash university or passed selection, but he was far from uneducated when it came to reading people. You might say he possessed a natural gift.

He eyeballed him, letting him feel the force of his contempt, then let his eyes settle down, taking the man in piece by piece. he carried a Vector 9mm full auto, and a secondary weapon - a Sig Saur .45 by the looks of it. Pretty fancy gear. No chance of them being a regular military unit, carrying kit like that. Which meant they were private contractors. But why?

"OK, you know my name. What's yours?" Fergie hissed.

The big man grinned and held up his hands.

"Well now, that would be telling, wouldn't it? Do you ever watch westerns? Well, let's just say I'm the man in black. The one everybody should be scared of."

"Oh yeah? Is that so? Well, cut the shit. I'd say you've made your point. What do you want and who sent you?"

Roberts took a final step forward, his hands resting casually on his weapon.

"Ah, goddamn, that's refreshing to hear; straight to the point. I can respect that. Just as much of a people person as your file suggests. Well, then, let's see. Firstly, I want world peace, and then an end to global warming. Promptly followed by a ban on rap music—I fucking hate that stuff. Oh, and the spear. I know that idiot academic had it, but he's dead, ergo, you are now in possession of it. Secondly, I want you and what's left of your team to come out with your hands up. How's that grab you?"

Fergie maintained eye contact; he didn't want to give this man the satisfaction of looking away.

"Spear? All this drama over that old piece of shite; have you got any idea what's happening out there? I hate to break it to you, tough guy, but you've got more important things to be worrying about than us. We should be working together."

The big man appeared unfazed.

"Sorry, old chum, but that's never gonna happen. I do indeed know what's happening—in fact, I know a damn sight more than you—but that's none of your concern. The grown-ups with deal with it. With regards to the aforementioned artefact, that piece of boot sale rubbish holds no more meaning to me than your life. My employer, however, seems to want it. Between you and me, I don't really care for him much either, but he does sign the paycheck. So, you know, 'Orders are orders'. I'm sure you know the score."

He hated the smarmy bastard already.

"I've a counter-offer. How about you and your goons turn around and fuck off, before I beat the living shite out of you. How's that grab ya, ya wee prick?" Fergie spat.

The big man shrugged his shoulders and lowered his head.

"You know, I had a funny feeling you were going to say something like that. And, to be brutally honest, I was kind of hoping you would. Look, one professional to another, there just isn't any room for tourists on this cruise. It's a stone cold fact that none of you will be leaving that building alive, But I'm not a monster. I don't want to hurt you more than necessary. So why not just give up and I promise to make it quick, single shot to the back of the head. Can't say fairer than that, eh?"

The blast from Downs' shotgun was monstrous.

"Fuck you!" he growled, and he let off another three shots, catching one of their attackers square in the chest; the force of the impact sent the man sprawling into a parked car, before slumping to the floor.

"Do it!" howled Roberts, as he dropped below the firing line. The road was suddenly alight with muzzle flashes and the glint of spent brass littering the wet tarmac. The Marines hit the floor as the fresh wave of bullets peppered the store.

Fergie, Downs and Libby held their ears, pinned down by the sheer rate of firepower. But, much to the Scotsman's surprise, it lasted mere seconds before something changed. Despite the sustained fracas, it became apparent that they were no longer the targets.

They began to hear screaming, mingled with the muffled shouts and intermittent gunshots. Fergie closed his eyes, straining to hear, for there was another noise growing in volume, a sound that cut through the storm, and sent a wave of fear through his body. It was the all-too-familiar sound of those nightmarish creatures.

He swallowed hard as the street began to pulse with the ominous green light and, glancing over the top, he caught a flash of movement leaping down from the building opposite. He looked up. The darkness was...rippling somehow, then, as if spewed from hell itself, he began to see blackened shapes, a multitude, crawling over the rooftops, their number growing with every passing second. Below them, the hit-squad had seen them too, their cries of warning morphing into screams of terror as the horde began to drop.

The night resonated with sporadic bursts of gunfire interspersed with torturous weeping as they began to lay waste to the hit-squad.

From just outside his field of vision came a gut-wrenching roar. The hulking frame of a troll filled the window, its gnarled fist dragging a huge axe along the pavement. Before it, a soldier began to back away emptying a full magazine into the monstrosity. The bullets had little effect. He turned and sprinted for the open shop window, choosing to take his chances with the Marines rather than the giant. With a deafening howl and an explosive crash, the monster swung its axe into the side of a parked car, which flew—as if it weighed no more than a child's toy—through the air to slam into the soldier. The impact of the twisted wreck was such that his legs were crushed against the wall. Unfortunately for him, the momentum threw the rest of his body over the sill and the glass it still held, slicing through stomach and spine. The upper torso toppled into the shop with a thud, gasping and scrabbling in helpless horror. Libby screamed long and loud.

Fergie didn't waste any time. He grabbed hold of Libby's hand and sprinted through the shop, followed closely by Titan and Downs. Behind them cam the sound of a mighty explosion. A grenade perhaps. With luck, it had brought the shop-front down, covering their escape.

They crashed through the basement doorway, down the stairs and across the cellar, relieved to have this means of escape. Fergie paused at the tunnel entrance to snatch up the rucksacks. He threw one to Downs, along with a fresh shotgun. They fastened the straps around their waists and checked their weapons. Downs gave a nod.

"All loaded and ready to rock, boss. We ain't got much time; those fuckers won't be far behind us. What's the plan at the other end?"

Fergie thumbed the switch of a torch, his hand shaking from the adrenaline. Breathing heavily, he swept the cavernous void before him, the arc of light swallowed by the gloom. He turned to address the others, his tone sombre yet commanding. He was scared—there was no denying it—but he had to keep his mind sharp, for all their sakes.

"I know we are all scared, angry, and those things ain't gonna stop coming for us while they've got out scent, but now is not the time to lose our shit. So, let's keep it together and keep our heads in the game. we'll go single file. Me first, Libby and Titan in the middle. Downs, you take the rear. Keep your eyes peeled; I don't want anything sneaking up on us. It's a short tunnel, but we know what's at the other end. We're going to vault the wall, and head down the alley. No heroics—and above all, we stay together. OK, let's go!" And one-by-one, they entered the darkness.

CHAPTER TWENTY THREE

It was cold down there. In fact, it was bloody freezing. The chill clawed at their bones. They kept moving, breath pluming as mist before them as they darted through the tunnel.

The shaft itself wasn't long, but it was cramped. Awkward. And the space didn't lend itself well to acoustics, so if a firefight did happen, the sound would be deafening. Common sense dictated that they should get out as quickly as possible.

"How far?" Libby whispered, her voice quavering.

Fergie turned and put his finger to his lips.

"Shh, not far," he whispered.

Behind them, Downs suddenly stopped. Fergie shone his torch towards the Marine, careful not to blind him.

"What's up?" he hissed.

"Dunno, thought I heard something, something moving."

Fergie snapped off the torch, took hold of Libby's shoulder, and gently pushed her behind him. He and Downs raised their weapons, scanning the darkness for any sign of pursuit. They stood motionless, breaths held.

"Well?" whispered Fergie. "Anything?"

Through the gloom, Fergie could just make out his comrade shaking his head.

"Sorry boss, nerves are fried. Don't like confined spaces."

"It's OK, mate. I'm on edge, too. Let's just get the hell out of here."

***

It only took a few more moments to reach the end of the tunnel. Fergie worked his way up a small flight of stone steps. Above him was a heavy wooden hatch. He gently nudged it with the barrel of his shotgun and winced at the creak. He peered out, rotating to take in all he could.

"How's it looking?" Downs whispered.

"All good. Trouble is, it may make a hell of a noise when we open it all the way. No way of knowing. Best get ready. Those things may be on us quick-smart."

Downs wiped his brow and hefted his shotgun, the weapon's weight reassuring in his grip.

"Well, let's get going then, the suspense is bloody killing me."

Quick or slow? Quick or slow? The Scotsman huffed and swept the hatch open, emerging with his gun at the ready. The creak was sharp but very short. Better than long and drawn-out. Less easy to catch amid the uproar out front. One by one they exited, keeping low, beneath the window of the small structure. Fergie signalled to Downs to go and check their route was clear.

"Are we safe now, Fergie?" Libby whispered.

"Not yet, sweetheart. But I'm working on it."

"Nothing will be the same again, will it?"

"Sure it will, hen. Things always get better. You just have to hang on sometimes."

The young girl snorted.

"Now you're just trying to make me feel better. I've seen what's out there."

The sudden shadow cast by Downs' return broke the awkward exchange and made Fergie's heart skip a beat.

"Sorry boss, didn't mean to scare you."

"Yeah, yeah. How's it looking?"

"Seems OK. Pretty big garden, overrun with weeds and full of junk. There's a small pile of stone slabs we can use to get over the wall. Seems pretty stable." Fergie pressed his face to the window and wiped a clean streak across the filthy pane. When so much was at stake, the burden of command was heavy: holding the lives of others in his hands—especially now a young girl had been thrown into the mix. *All alone now, like Smudger's Stacy.*

"Well?" asked Libby, her hands buried in Titan's fur. "Are the monsters out there?"

Fergie hefted his weapon and smiled softly.

"If there are, I'll make sure they don't bother you. How's that?"

The young girl smiled and raised her arm, her 'magic sword' clasped tightly. in her hand. The appearance of the long knife caught both men by surprise.

"You two aren't the only ones who can fight. Titan and I will help."

Downs laughed softly, shaking his head at the little girl's audacity.

"Well then, young lady. In that case, let's go monster-hunting!"

Downs went first this time, weapon primed, nipping over to the neatly-piled stack of slabs. He climbed to the top and peeked over. Clear, he signalled. Fergie gave a sharp nod, and Downs disappeared from view. Fergie sent Libby next. To his surprise, she climbed with supreme confidence and dropped down the other side with barely a pause. No fear in that one. He wondered then if he'd have to carry the dog, but Titan raced past him, up and over before he could blink. By contrast, the Scotsman had to drag himself over, landing with a hard thump on the concrete below.

The others had their bodies pressed up against the far wall, reducing their profiles should anything pass the alley's mouth.

"Which way?" Downs hissed.

Fergie pointed up the alleyway to his left.

"Let's move slow and steady. I'll take point, Libby and Titan in the middle again. Let's just clear the area for now."

As they reached the end of the alleyway, they paused, ducking behind a large delivery truck parked up on the curb, its doors flung wide, the dirty windows splattered with blood. Fergie gave the cab a cursory glance, then peered around the bonnet, studying the high street. His breath caught at the devastation before him.

Off to their right, he noted the road rose on a slight gradient then disappeared to the left in a dogleg. To their left, the beginnings of the road that the gun shop had once been on.

"Well, I reckon we've got no choice but to head up the high street, but it ain't pretty."

Downs peered past him. "Pretty? Shit, boss, it's a slaughterhouse out there. Why do they do that then bugger off? What's their game?"

"No idea, mate, but I don't give a shite, as long as they're away from us." Fergie got to his feet.

"Come on, let's get moving. We'll find ourselves a good strong base, another church maybe, rest up for a bit, and plan our next move. Figure out how to draw the hell-bitch out."

After a final inspection of the area, they moved forward cautiously, manoeuvring their way up the high street between the burning wreckage and bloody remains.

***

His vantage point was pretty much perfect. In the distance, he could see the thick plumes of acrid smoke rising from fires that still raged in the once-beautiful buildings. Above him, swimming through the storm, monstrous shapes wove between angry clouds, all smoke and pockets of green light. It was a scene from the worst kind of nightmare.

Roberts had managed to slip away as shortly after the firefight started. It didn't take long to realise his men were hopelessly outmatched and he wasn't stupid enough to go down fighting for a shit-stain like Sir Malcolm Hawker. In all his years of service, he had never encountered so formidable a foe. These fairy folk, not the knight. And to be honest, that unnerved him. He and his men were professionals. Soldiers at the very top of their game. The elite. Yet, they were torn apart in a matter of minutes.

While retreating, he had witnessed one of his men battling to the last and, with his final breath, he'd take some of those bastards with him. Devlin's final act was one of bravery and self-sacrifice, but Roberts had cursed him anyway. The grenade had almost caught him too, and that would have been a fucking crime. A parked car had fortunately taken the brunt of the blast, leaving him with only a mild concussion. He'd managed to stumble a little way down the road undetected, ducking into the first secure building he encountered.

High ground, that was the key. Common sense when dealing with two enemies, each posing different threat levels. He knew damn well there was no fight to be had with the creatures at this moment in time: he wouldn't last two minutes on his own and in this state. His primary targets were something more manageable. In fact, to him, it was now more than just a job. It was personal. Directly or not, Ferguson and his merry band of cronies were responsible for the deaths of his men, some of whom had been good friends. It was down to the Scotsman that his mission had descended into chaos, and he was going to pay for that. As luck would have it, Roberts wouldn't have to wait very long for a second chance. A chance to even the score.

He smiled as he focused his high-res binoculars and watched the three figures moving up the high street, their bodies hugging the edge of the buildings, hoping to evade detection.

He sat back, retrieved a small radio from his jacket pocket and thumbed the switch, a hiss of static in his earpiece.

"Charlie One, receive. This is Falcon. Over."

"Falcon, Charlie One, received. Go for SITREP. Over."

"Team is down. Incursion force substantial. Reset to Incursion level one. Request immediate containment. I repeat. Request immediate containment. Over."

A slight pause and a sharp hiss of static.

"Falcon. Status on primary understood. Request status of secondary target. Over."

Roberts gritted his teeth. The bastards pulling the strings didn't give a shit that his men were dead. That he could have died. This was why he'd gone private in the first place. He gripped the radio, temper rising, his hand aching with the pressure.

"Secondary in the wind. Eyes on, and about to follow. Over," he hissed.

Another short pause.

"Understood, Falcon. Follow, engage, terminate. Check-in when complete, EVAQ LZ to be determined. Over and out."

The radio went dead.

"Spineless cunt," he growled, as he replaced the comms unit.

He got to his feet, slung his backpack, and secured his gear. He eyed the war-ravaged high street and the shadows skulking from building-to-building.

"You'd better pray those things find you first, Ferguson," he whispered as he primed his weapon.

"Because I'm coming for you."

CHAPTER TWENTY FOUR

To Fergie's surprise and delight, they made it to the church unhindered and with zero contact with any of the creatures. This, of course, was more than a little unnerving. Where was the local response? How could so much carnage be wrought without consequence, and how did the horde vanish so completely? Not to mention the she-witch herself —surely she was still out there, in the darkness? What was her game? What did she actually want? He rubbed his face, trying to rid himself of these troubling thoughts. For now, he was simply glad of the respite. He shook his head and returned his attention to the gloom-shrouded church across the street; an island of calm, afloat in a sea of devastation.

"Looks clear. What d'ya reckon?"

Downs took in the surroundings. The road in both directions, the narrow lanes scattered with smouldering cars and blood-soaked litter. He sighed deeply, his shaking hands clasping his shotgun.

"Um, well, we really ain't got much of a choice. It's the best option so far. We are too exposed out here. To be honest guv, I'm scared shitless."

"OK, then. Fuck it, we're going in. Stay sharp and watch our backs, we're nearly at the finish line."

Fergie held up three fingers and counted down. Both men brought their weapons up to their shoulders. On a clenched fist, they sprang to their feet and, with Libby and Titan wedged between them, sprinted towards the church. In a fluid motion, they crossed the road, dodged through the small gate and flowed up the path to the great church doors. The door was unlocked, much to their relief. A true sanctuary, then. After a quick look over his shoulder Fergie pulled open the door and they entered, weapons sweeping the darkness.

They gently closed the door and secured it with the heavy iron key Fergie found on a hook nearby. The main room was of a decent size, its ceiling high. The entire width of the building was crossed with large pine beams, secured by thick iron rivets. The walls were light and airy, not at all like the oppressive stone buildings Fergie had visited before, and certainly a lot more welcoming than the last place. This was a progressive church, a revamp to entice a new generation of followers into the fold.

"What the hell is with us and bloody churches?" asked Downs.

Fergie chortled.

"Dunno, mate. But we need all the help we can get, wouldn't you say?"

"Didn't help us last time, did it? Didn't help the Sarge."

"No. It didn't," he growled, pushing his feelings back down. He wasn't ready to face that guilt. Not yet. Not while the threat still loomed large. Cursing himself and his big mouth, Downs ruffled Titan's fur. Libby looked up at him.

"What's the plan?" she asked.

"Well, young lady, the first thing we do is to give the place a proper sweep; make sure no bad guys are hiding. Then, we'll set up some defences, and *you*—" he bopped her playfully on the nose,"—are gonna get some kip."

Her smile was infectious, a shining beacon in the storm.

"Come on. Let's crack on," he said.

***

For the next twenty minutes, they managed to fortify the entrances, the front and inner doors barricaded with pews and other ornate furniture; they used a large crucifix as a wedge, should the locks fail. They covered the two low-level stained-glass windows with heavy drapes and secured them with string and cords.

The place was no fortress, but it'd do. A modern church with minimal entry points. Even the small rooms to the rear were either windowless or secure by default due to the tiny windows. Fergie insisted they were to be secured nonetheless. But there was a downside to the increased security. If they should be overrun, the chances of escape were slim. There was no escape route, no back-up plan. They had to hope the rest of the long night would pass without them being discovered; use the daylight hours to rouse help.

Libby had ventured off to explore their temporary home and had managed to find some blankets in a donation box for the local homeless community. She took great care to fold and prepare them, ready for the bustling Marines once they had finished their tasks. Fergie, meanwhile, had located a small kitchen and returned triumphantly with a box full of chocolate bars, biscuits, and cans of pop to supplement the rations in their rucksacks. *The beginnings of a feast,* he mused. Not to mention a wind-up radio, though, despite Downs' best efforts, all they could hear was the harsh screech of static. Still no signals getting through... Before long, a makeshift recreation area had been constructed with Libby now curled up and fast asleep, the ever-loyal Titan at her feet. Fergie and Downs had watched her for a few minutes, each lost to their own thoughts.

In the end, Downs broke the silence. "We gotta make things right, Ferg. We gotta make sure the world knows the truth about all this."

The Scotsman shook his head slowly and adjusted his position, his face creasing with concern.

"One thing at a time, Stevie. We have to survive the night first. But say we do. Say we find a way to stop the Huldra and those beasties. Do you think for one minute that the people out there in 'normal' land will believe us? The powers that be will come up with a cover story and the public will buy it. Hell, all they have to do is say there was some kind of toxic spill or contamination caused by the storm—maybe a nuclear meltdown. There are loads of facilities nearby to pin the blame on. I can see them on the news already: 'So sorry all those people died. It was a tragic accident brought on by the weather. Thoughts and prayers. In other news..."

"People would ask questions though, surely?" asked Downs, suddenly sounding very young. Fuck. Poor kid. And he was a kid really, when all was said and done. Young and dumb.

"Mate, they can ask as many questions as they want, doesn't mean they're going to get the right answers. Haven't you heard of False Flag operations? All governments get up to shady stuff, ours ain't no different. They can't exactly come out on live TV and say that an ancient evil leading an unstoppable horde was resurrected and went on the rampage, can they? So, they got to cover their tracks. Social media and all its fake news is a big thing. You can bet your ass they'll use that to their advantage. Control the story and you control reality. It doesnae matter if it's true or not."

Deflated and confused, Downs slumped backwards, lost in thought, chewing the remnants of his chocolate bar. After a few minutes thinking it over, Downs asked the question Fergie dreaded. The one that left them cornered. "OK, boss, where does that leave us? You and me? If we actually manage to survive this, I mean. The Sarge and the others, they deserve fucking medals. The world should know what they did, what they sacrificed."

"I agree. Our lads died defending us, and for that they should acknowledged, avenged. But I'll tell you this," and here Fergie jabbed an angry finger out at the town, "that bastard and his goons weren't regular army—I doubt they were even Special Forces. Want my take on 'em? They were private contractors, taking orders from someone else. Someone powerful, with deep pockets. You see the kit they were packing? We must really be a major pain in the arse for them to send in a kill squad, and on British soil, no less. Trust me, mate, they have no intention of leaving any loose ends.

Downs was caught somewhere between terror and outrage. It came to Fergie again just how young and innocent the lad was. Aye, and how young Collins had been, and O'Hagan. Brewer. Christ, Smudger hadn't been all that old. "At the end of the day," he sighed, "all I'm concerned with is keeping us all alive through the night. Get to sunrise and we have a chance. I'll worry about those responsible later. Whoever they turn out to be."

Downs brooded on this, kick his heels and gnawing at his thumbnail. The cruelty of it all, the carelessness with which their lives had been deemed disposable just ate him up. "Gotta go for a slash. Be right back."

Fergie watched him disappear through the back. The lad was right. It was fucking unfair.

He reached inside his jacket and retrieved the spearhead, turning it over in his hands. He marvelled at how sharp the tip was, even after all these years. It was ice-cold to the touch. He thought back to Brewer, the stuffy nerd who'd started all this. He'd seemed so sure the spear was key to defeating the Huldra, and with all they'd seen tonight, they'd started to buy it. He snorted. To think he'd imagined luring her out so he could stab her with it—as if he could even get close. As if her death would make the rest of the horde just disappear. As if he was the Hunter and not her.

The realisation hit home like a sledgehammer, the cold, stark truth now shockingly obvious. It was a trap: the Huldra knew precisely where they were. Of course she did. She had been toying with them all along, corralling her prey towards the kill-zone. He moved to Libby's side and gently shook her awake. She peered up at him through sleep-encrusted eyes.

"What's up, Fergie?" she croaked.

"Get up, Blue-eyes. We've gotta go, now!"

He tucked the spear away, picked up the shotgun and made for the back to fetch Downs. Behind him, Libby was slipping on her shoes. Titan growled suddenly, the echo shockingly loud. And then the world stopped.

"We meet again, warrior."

The voice sent a chill through Fergie's body Standing before him was the Huldra, withered arms outstretched as if to embrace him, or hanging perhaps on an invisible cross. He found his eyes drawn inexorably towards her own, barely taking in her distorted features or skeletal body. Only her eyes seemed alive. She was amused.

"I have enjoyed our little game this evening," she smiled. "It's been such an honour to have you partake. You and your warband have proved worthy adversaries, so, I shall give you the chance to join the hunt of your own free will. Yours will be glory and renown, the finest of weapons, and honoured place at the feasting board. Or... we can take you. What's left won't be much good, I'm afraid. You'd be more like the hound than the Hunter, but we'll find some use for you, I'm sure. What say you?"

The shotgun was fully loaded: ten rounds, one in the chamber, ready to go. The thought barely crossed his mind when he saw it, held carelessly in her hand. She flashed a wicked grin as his eyes widened.

"Ah, yes. I forgot. I found your little friend." Fergie watched on in horror as the severed head tumbled through the air and landed with a wet thump at his feet. He felt something like pain in his chest, and Fergie wondered briefly if he was having a heart attack. He felt cold there. Icy. But no pain, strangely. It was then he remembered the spear, tucked safely once more in his jacket; It matched the shape of the cold. Not a heart attack. He smiled, the beginnings of a plan fermenting.

"The big, bad Huldra, eh? Top of the fucking food chain, and leader of the Wild Hunt. You...are the leader, right? While the cat's away, at least. Bless. Well, let me give you some advice: you're not in the Viking age now, bitch, and we ain't packing swords."

His movements were blisteringly fast, raising the shotgun and blasting it off, five shots slamming into the Huldra's chest. The impact sending her sprawling backwards and heard himself screaming "Fuck you!"— spitting with rage as her pellet-riddled body hit the stone flagging.

He emptied another five rounds directly into her, moving towards her all the while, keeping her down. As the last shot hit home, he discarded the gun and reached under his jacket, pulling the spearhead free. His hand burned now with the cold of it as he raised it high, poised to put an end to her.

And that's when Libby shrieked.

***

He swallowed hard. Mere seconds had passed but the moment was lost. He looked about him. How quickly a battle could turn. The room was full of creatures. Wiry, feline beasts hanging from the rafters; dwarves at the doors; beside them, resting against the walls, colossal trolls. And now, as he completed his slow three sixty, he noted a gathering of long-dead Viking warriors, come to flank the Huldra, their ancient weapons at the ready. Libby ran over, threw her arms around him, and began to weep uncontrollably.

The Scotsman pocketed the artefact, snatched up the shotgun and began to thumb in his last ten cartridges. He pulled back the charging handle and released, loading the first round.

"Come now, did you really think you could defeat me,

warrior?"

She sat up with a lazy smile and looked down at her chest. The marks of his attack dissipated at her touch. Fergie lowered his head and began to stroke Libby's hair.

"Don't look, sweetheart. It will all be over soon. Just... keep your eyes closed for me, OK?"

The young girl nodded, her face buried in the Scotsman's thigh as the wild huntress began to climb to her feet once more. The sudden flash of movement caught him by surprise. In fact, no one in the room realised what was happening until it was too late. Titan lunged forward, launching himself at the Huldra with a vicious snarl, his powerful jaws clamping around her face. There was a sickening ripping sound as his teeth tore through skin and muscle. She let out a shriek as she fell backwards beneath the savage dog.

Libby screamed at the horrible sounds, but Fergie held her firm, bringing the shotgun up and pointing it at the nearest beast, its gaping mouth thick with saliva.

The point-blank blast was glorious. Devastating. The creature's head exploded like an overripe watermelon. Fergie swung the weapon skyward and pulled the trigger. A deafening blast. The punishing recoil. Another creature dropping, this time from the rafters. They began to close in around them, a hate-filled pack intent on feasting upon their bones. Once again, he hefted the shotgun, and once again, the load found its mark. He could hardly miss.

Libby clung to him, her sobs lost within the cacophony of snarls and gunfire. But as Fergie freed the beast within, ready to go down fighting, another sound caught his attention. It was a metallic clinking, like a can tumbling across the pavement in the wind. And the room was suddenly drenched in a brilliant white flash. A great boom resounded. He raised his hand to his face and tucked downwards over Libby, his senses overloaded by a high-pitched whine. The foul beasts also fell into disorientation, their limbs flailing, their eyes burning from the unexpected detonation.

"Fergie!" cried Libby, her arms still locked around his waist as he began to stumble forward. He shook his head, rubbed at his eyes, tried desperately to regain some sense of equilibrium in the aftermath of the stun grenade. Roberts! It had to be.

His vision began to clear, the air around him filled with growls and chaotic screeches. He hefted the shotgun, ready to fire its final round, as a blackened form began to bound towards him. But before he could identify a target, another sound reverberated, along with guttural screams of disbelief. The horde began to scatter.

Fergie spun on his heels, and saw, though stinging eyes, the figure of Roberts charging through the doors of the church, his rifle at his shoulder, spitting venom, dropping abominations on all sides.

"Ferguson!" he bellowed as he turned his weapon on the Marine and squeezed the trigger. Fergie threw himself to the floor, Libby at his side, and his shotgun slid from his grasp. A wave of gunshots shattered the air above them.

"What the fuck are you doing?" he rasped, as the nut job slammed home a fresh magazine.

"I'm coming for ya, Jock!" Another volley of rounds hammered out, keeping the creatures back.

"For Christ's sake, man, there's a child here!"

"I don't care!" he screamed, his hand fumbling for a fresh mag.

Roberts pushed forward, his body hunched. He spun left and opened fire, ripping through a troll's face, then right, as a skinny feral-looking creature launched itself skyward. Roberts didn't flinch; his weapon followed and found its mark.

Libby was curled up behind a pew, covered in splintered wood and dust. She looked up at her protector but said nothing, her eyes conveying her fear, begging him to remain with her. But he couldn't do that.

"Stay here!" he ordered, clenching his fists and lunging towards Roberts.

CHAPTER TWENTY FIVE

Fergie motored forward, throwing himself into a rugby tackle. The impact of the collision sent both men sprawling backwards in a heap of twisted limbs and flailing punches. Roberts lashed out but he couldn't gain traction, his swings useless in close proximity. Together, they rolled. Fergie's head slammed into the stone flooring, the jarring impact causing his vision to flicker with streaks of white light. Blindly, he dug his fist upwards, connecting with soft tissue. Balls were too much to hope for; stomach was more likely. Using all his strength, he pushed himself away, rolling free. He managed to get to his feet first and immediately threw a savage kick, sending the downed man's weapon skidding across the floor and disappearing beneath the horde creatures.

There was a throaty growl from various creatures, and Fergie had to look at them twice. Were they... just watching? Taking fucking bets? Was this just entertainment for them? Fergie threw a massive right hook—but Roberts was moving, regaining his feet; he sidestepped and threw a strike of his own, smashing his fist into Fergie's jaw. Stars exploded and he stumbled backwards, shaken by the surprisingly heavy blow. The odious private contractor adopted a boxing stance, fluid and mobile, shifting his shoulders in readiness.

"Is that all you've got, Scot?" he growled, and he threw a lightning combination, one-two-three, that left him reeling. It was brutal.

"I thought Royal Marines were supposed to be tough guys," he bellowed. "You ain't nothing!" And he darted in with another devastating combo.

Fergie's head rolled backwards, his legs buckled

beneath him, and he dropped. His head was thumping. He was half-blind with the pain—or was it blood? Roberts waded in with a kick to the head. Arrogantly telegraphed. Fergie spotted it coming and dipped to one side, catching hold of the incoming extremity. He lashed up at Roberts' exposed groin, once, twice with his heavy boot, and smiled as the colour drained from the bastard's face. Roberts looked like he was going to cough. Throw up. Faint maybe.

Fergie took the opportunity to get up once more. He was never a nimble man but he could shift when he had to. He took a step inwards and landed a heavy blow of his own, relishing the savage crack as Roberts' nose broke under it.

"I'm just getting started, cunt," he shouted. "Come on!" But as he stepped forward, he saw his opponent draw and level his pistol. Fergie dived headlong as Roberts let off three rounds. Two missed him, slamming into something behind that hissed and spat in pain, but that was by and by. Fergie grunted as the third bullet struck his shoulder, sending him crashing to the floor. Roberts let out a roar to the onlookers, then his shifted his weapon to a two-handed tactical grip and fired again.

All the Scotsman could do was roll his body, once, twice, his shoulder an agony. Chips flew up from the ground behind him. Running on pure adrenaline, he rose to his feet, as gunfire snapped again. It was then that he realised, much to his relief, that it wasn't directed at him. The horde had had enough fun. With the bullets flying once more, and their members taking strays, it was time to bring their prey to ground. Roberts emptied his magazine into a pair of cat-like creatures bearing down on him. Fergie didn't waste a second. He rounded the upturned pew and, dropping to his knees, was relieved to see her sweet face looking up at him.

"Libby! You OK?" he asked, checking her for any apparent injuries.

"I stayed hidden. You don't look so good." She reached up her hand to his eye. He jerked his head away.

"I'm peachy. Come on, we're leaving."

Fergie held out his hand and she took it. He pulled her to her feet and retrieved the shotgun.

They peered from behind the splintered wood to see the contractor putting two more rounds into a dying horror. There was something almost pitiful about it, like a mouse surrounded by cats. He might get the odd bite in, but they'd grow tired of the game soon enough. And then he'd be done.

It was then that Fergie sensed another foe, close behind. The swish of a robe as she struck was all the warning he got before the Huldra struck. Libby screamed shrilly as her guardian was tossed through the air like a rag doll, crashing into the wall and dropping heavily to the ground. The Huldra looked down at her and smiled and reached out a hand to cup her chin gently.

"You're a pretty little one. Such beautiful blue eyes."

Libby practically fell backwards in her desperation to get away, batting the Huldra's delicate fingers away and scrambling back. The creature's laughter was eerie amidst the carnage. "Run then, child. I'll catch you soon."

On the far side of the room, Fergie stirred. Libby was shaking his shoulders, sobbing and desperate to shift him. His vision swam. The sounds all around were muggy and disjointed.

"Fergie! Fergie!"

An arrow shattered on the wall by his head, startling them both. They ducked for cover as more fell about them. Bastards!

"Where's Titan?" screamed Libby, her face stained with tears and dirt.

Fergie knew they had little time; he gripped her tighter and pulled her close. The lie came so easy it might have been truth. "Titan's gone. He got away, but we've got to go too now. Come on!" Together, hand-in-hand, they ran, lungs screaming for oxygen as they made for the front door, their bodies low. Behind them, another deafening blast of gunfire rang out as the contractor defended his position, spitting impotent cries of rage and fear.

Roberts felt the slide lock back, his final rounds used up. He tossed the gun and retrieved his final grenade from his pocket, pulling the pin with a snarl. The spoon disengaged with a springy chime as the black sphere flew. It bounced and rolled along the stone flooring, coming to rest beneath an enormous troll. It looked down just as the grenade detonated, taking it off its feet and into the wall, its chest and face reduced to pulp.

Amidst the smoke and swirling debris, Roberts tried to stand, but his legs were unresponsive. The only thing he could do was drag himself backwards on his hands, scanning the floor for any sort of weapon. It was then he caught sight of his Vector 9mm lying where that lanky bastard had kicked it. He began to crawl towards the gun, his limbs burning from the exertion, a trail of blood smearing the floor. With a painful scream, he felt two arrows slam into his body: one in his shoulder, the other in his lower back. They burned like fire. He kept moving, his bloodied hand reaching for the discarded weapon.

Kneeling beside him, the Huldra extended her skeletal hand, wisps of flesh hanging uselessly from her blackened bones. The foul stench of decay filled the downed man's nostrils.

"It's time," she cackled, reaching out and stroking his hair. Her viking warriors came in close, eager to see the unholy rite.

Roberts gripped the sub-machine gun and rolled onto his back, a surge of agony shredding his nerves as one of the arrows snapped beneath him. His trigger finger clench with the pain and raised the gun, dumping thirteen rounds right into the Huldra's face. There was an ungodly roar as the thing fell back, and her minions letting out cries of shock. Then, as the gun emptied and its echoes died, their shock turned to anger. And as one, they fell upon him.

***

They were everywhere now; the rooftops were a swirling sea of atrocities, all closing in on the damned church. The black sky above split over and over with tendrils of green, each heralding new arrivals.

Fergie dared not linger. In desperation, he scanned the war-ravaged street. Many of the surrounding buildings were now ablaze, belching smoke into the sky. He imagined families suffocating in their sleep, snuffed out—unaware of their passing, let alone the horrors that brought it about. He envied them that, in a way. Then, to his right, His eyes came to rest on a flatbed truck discarded half on the pavement. The driver's door hung wide open. He ran towards it, the night echoing with rapturous screams. And as they leapt in, the church doorway opened, spewing forth a swarm of hungry creatures.

He slammed the door and locked it, then snatched at the ignition. Libby scrabbled to get her seat belt on, still sobbing for Titan. The truck spluttered, then burst into life. In that moment of fierce triumph, the first wave hit the back of the truck, causing the heavy vehicle to rock violently.

"Hold on!" he yelled, gunning the accelerator. The vehicle shuddered and lurched forward, the offside wheels bouncing from the curb and spinning until they found purchase through the remnants of the previous owner. Behind them, several creatures had leapt aboard the flatbed and one lashed out, smashing the back window. Libby screamed as the glass imploded, showering them both with tiny fragments. Fergie kept his eyes focused ahead but he jerked the wheel violently, while at the same time yanking the handbrake. In a hideous screech of tyres, the vehicle slid sideways, the back end juddering to a violent and sudden stop. The momentum flung their attackers from the flatbed, straight through a shop window. Fergie slammed the vehicle into reverse as one of the creatures rose to its feet, ready to attack again, but the pick-up rocketed backwards and hit it full-force, knocking it down and crushing it underneath.

Libby hollered a warning as Fergie struggled to get it into first, the gears grinding horribly. The horde was bearing down on them once more. With a whine, the gearbox suddenly engaged, and the small truck shot forward. Fergie spun the wheel, causing the vehicle to fishtail horribly.

"How close are they?" he demanded, as they began to pick up speed. Libby gripped on to the back of the seat, peering out through the rain.

"They're falling behind, but keep going! Keep going!"

"Good. Keep watching, tell me when we're clear."

It was then the monstrously large troll stepped from the shadows, its axe already in mid-swing. Fergie snatched the wheel, causing the truck to veer violently to the left. Libby grabbed hold of the dashboard and pushed back in her seat as they sideswiped a Mercedes. Fergie spun the wheel again, pulling it to the right this time. The metal-on-metal collision raked at his ears. By some miracle, the brutal axe blade sailed behind the cab, missing by inches, though they'd never know it. Fergie glanced in the mirror and held his breath as the Mercedes took the hit, lifted by the force of that terrible blow and tossed into the second storey of the building opposite. As its fuel tank ruptured, the once-valuable car exploded in a searing fireball.

The troll reversed its swing, the flames silhouetting its body, and Fergie's eyes widened. He could see what was coming.

"Move, god damn it!" he roared as the lumbering beast released the axe. Libby screamed as the projectile flew through the air, a spinning tirade of flame and vengeance.

With his peripheral vision, the Scotsman caught sight of the weapon spinning past the driver's window, then with an explosive crash, it it struck a double-decker bus ahead of them. The robust vehicle was taken off its wheels and onto its side by the sheer power of the impact, its windows imploding as it slammed to the tarmac.

"Keep down!" he growled, and they sped away, leaving the monster far behind.

***

"Where are we going, Fergie?"

Fergie kept his eyes on the road. His mind was racing. One by one his options had been stripped away. *Where were they going?* How the fuck would he know?

"We can't drive too far in these floods. This truck's nice and high, but it isn't a boat. And we still need to find my mum," the young girl added, almost apologetically. Her voice broke on that last word, and she curled up. Poor lass.

The cold, hard facts were simple. She was right; there was no way they could escape the area by road, and trying to make it on foot would be suicidal. They'd already tried to find and hunker down in a few well-fortified buildings, hoping to stay hidden until morning, but the Huldra always seemed to know their whereabouts. Going to ground just played into her hands.

Back in the church, he'd missed the opportunity to kill the Huldra. He doubted he would get another one. She knew he had the spearhead now. The other thing he had to consider—a *good* thing—was that the team sent after him must have had an extraction plan. That meant a designated landing zone. Given the terrain, an EVAQ by chopper would be the easiest, but perhaps unlikely due to the storm front. For now, all he knew was that he had to keep the young girl safe; his own life was secondary.

He caught a fleeting glimpse of the moon, partially obscured by a solitary building up atop a large hill, the peak of which dominated the skyline.

"Libby, what's that there, up on the hill?"

The young girl turned and peered through the windscreen.

"That's not a hill, it's the Tor. The building on top is St Michael's tower; you must have heard of it! It's a horrible long walk up there." She wrinkled her nose and looked back at him, full of suspicion. "Why?"

For the first time in hours, Fergie felt a pang of hope. He turned to Libby.

"Because, young lady, I've got a plan."

CHAPTER TWENTY SIX

It took all of five minutes to reach the outskirts of town. Fergie abandoned the truck in a small car park at the base of the Tor. There was nothing of any use to be found in the truck, sadly. He'd had a good dig around. On the upside, he did find two fresh cartridges tucked away in his gear. It wasn't much, but it beat an empty weapon any day. And, should the worst come to the worst, at least he could spare Libby from—no. He squashed the thought down.

"Why are we going up the Tor?" whispered Libby. "Wouldn't it be better to hide inside somewhere?"

"Well, Marine Hooper, it's like this. We need a good vantage point, a place where we can see them coming, d'ya understand? Now, granted, they still have the cover of darkness, but my hope is that they'll expect us to hide up in town again. It might buy us some time, at any rate, and that's something we could do with right now. Even if the Huldra can track us, it may take her a while to get out here. She may be having too much fun in town to bother. Anyway, we have about two hours to sunrise; if we can hold out until then, we might be able to see a way out. I know it isn't the strongest plan, but it's all I've got for now. Do you trust me?"

Libby gave him a hug, her arms tight around his body.

"Of course I trust you. I know you're trying your best. Where you go, I go."

Fergie felt his heart swell. Her courage was unshakeable. He rose to his feet and tapped her on her head.

"Right, enough of the chit-chat. Are you ready to move,

Marine?'

Libby straightened up and saluted.

"Yes, sir."

He thumbed his final two rounds into the shotgun, cocked the weapon and cradled it in his arms.

"Right then, let's get going." And they started up the narrow gravel track snaking its way into darkness.

**

The wisp of green light flickered softly beneath the abandoned truck, its intensity pulsing and growing as it moved from the shadows out onto open ground. Its ethereal shape contorted as grew, illuminating the car park. It began to move, slowly at first as though seeking a scent, then with some speed towards the gravel track. It could see the shapes of its quarry now up ahead: one large, one small, each focused on the trail ahead. Somehow, they felt familiar; connected.

For half an hour, it stalked its prey, keeping always at a distance. No need to alert them to its presence. And now it knew where they were going, its mission was complete. The thing turned and sped down the hill, Flowing through earth and water, skimming past burning cars and ravaged corpses, eager to please its master.

The Huldra stood motionless in the road, the buildings of Glastonbury ablaze all around her; the horde busy at play. The illumination approached her, its head lowered in reverence, then stopped at her feet and whined with devotion. She smiled at the green spectral form of Titan then drank in all he'd seen.

"Good boy," she whispered.

**

It had taken them only thirty minutes to scale the Tor and Fergie was impressed by the young girl's pace. She'd had a little sleep in the church but really, she must be exhausted! Of course, he had deliberately held back a little, but she'd displayed considerable grit. He felt like a proud parent, basking in his daughter's accomplishments.

Fortunately, the place was devoid of creatures. Once the roofless building and it's surroundings had been secured, they stood silently together, their hands in their pockets for warmth.

Neither spoke a word as they took in their surroundings. The town below seemed an apocalyptic vision of burning fires, choking smoke, and battle-ravaged humanity. Further out, encircling the small town for miles, lay a vast temporary ocean, covering the once-fertile land. Flickers of light danced upon the surface still whipped by the winds and rain. He had witnessed many conflicts, walked the streets of many a war-zone, but he'd seen nothing to compare with tonight.

Libby reached out a trembling hand and took hold of Fergie's, her gaze never leaving the portrait of devastation.

"The world will be a very different place now," she whispered.

The Scotsman didn't respond at first, his mind a whirlwind of uncertainty.

"Libby," he said eventually, "I couldn't agree more. In fact, I think you may just be the smartest young lady I've ever had the pleasure of meeting." His stoic optimism was all but gone.

"Fergie? Do you think my mum is really out there? Or do you think she is dead? Please don't lie to make me feel better; tell me the truth."

Fergie shook his head. "I don't know. I honestly don't. So many innocent lives have been lost tonight. Perhaps she managed to hide. She may be at home now, waiting for you. She may...not. I'm sorry. I just don't have the answers."

The young girl nodded sombrely.

"That's what I was thinking. If she is alive, I'm sure she is hiding somewhere. She's way smarter than those things. But I have a feeling she's gone, and that makes me sad."

Fergie could feel himself choking up, and he stood there for a moment longer, shoulders shaking, holding it in as much as he could. He couldn't afford to let the dam break yet. They squeezed each other's fingers and watched the flames flickering below.

***

The tower itself wasn't that big but it appeared to have once had three levels. Its top was now roofless, the windows long gone. The area within was small but relatively secure, and, in truth, was the best they could make of a bad situation.

They sat themselves down on a small wooden bench, its planks marked by the passage of time, panels full of scratched messages by visiting tourists who wanted to leave their mark. Even the walls were covered with the prayers of wandering pilgrims.

"There's a lot of myth and history surrounding this place," said Libby, making herself comfortable.

"Oh yeah? Enlighten me. Might as well learn something while we're here."

"You make me laugh, Fergie, that's why I like you," Libby chuckled.

"Well, the pagans think that Morgan Le Fey lies beneath it—she was a sorceress—and they say it's the gateway to another world. Some say it's good, others say it's bad. And some people say it's the resting place of the Holy Grail, but I know that's not right."

"Oh yeah, why not?"

Libby let out another giggle.

"Because it's kept in a safe place in London, silly. Everybody knows that!"

"Oh, right. Sorry, my mistake. Please continue."

"In ancient times, they called this place The Isle of Avalon, because it looked like it lay in a sea of clouds. There isn't anything supernatural about that, though. It's just an optical illusion caused by air particles and varying temperatures. You know, because of the high moisture on The Levels."

"Flipping heck," said Fergie, "you really are a right little brainbox. Where did you learn all this stuff?"

"I like to read, especially about the area I live in. My mum used to like reading, too."

She gazed at the floor. Fergie sensed her unease and hugged her. She murmured something into his chest, but he couldn't hear her.

"What's that, lass?"

She pulled back and looked up at him seriously. "I said I keep thinking that... Well, if it wasn't for me, you could have killed the witch back in the church, and this would all be over. And Titan might be safe with us and—"

"Don't be a daftie. Look, hopefully we won't be seeing her again. You're a special wee girl. I can't even read or write, and boy, you should hear me do my times tables. Very embarrassing!" he quipped. She playfully punched him on the arm. He recoiled, feigning injury.

"Hey, that hurt, ya bully!"

She did it for a second time, harder, her face radiant with childish exuberance.

"Thanks again for looking after me," she whispered.

"You're welcome, Libby. I couldn't let you kill all those monsters on your own, could I?"

There was a moment of silence.

"Hey. To show your thanks for savin' yer butt, maybe you could teach me to read one day—how's that sound?" They both began to laugh, tears staining their grimy, dirt-covered faces.

It was then, caught in the briefest moment of joy, they heard her voice, ethereal in this place, resonating from the stone walls. The atmosphere chilled palpably and Fergie's chest tightened.

Fergie jumped to his feet, the shotgun swinging up to his shoulder. He tucked Libby behind him and edged forward, sweeping his gaze around as he approached the doorway. He braced himself against the side wall, ready to engage. Libby kept close behind, her breath coming in short gasps. She grabbed hold of his thigh, her hands trembling. She had to be brave.

The Scotsman couldn't hear any movement, nor could he set eyes on anything from his position. To gain visual, he had no other choice but to step outside.

He waved his hand, signalling her to remain still.

"Whatever you see, whatever you hear, you stay put, understand?" Libby shook her head in disagreement.

"No, don't go! Please don't leave me," she whimpered, clutching at his hand.

The Marine pulled his hand free, his face stern.

"You do as you're told, Marine. Do not follow me; that's an order." He turned swiftly on his heels then, and stepped out from the shadows.

CHAPTER TWENTY SEVEN

Sir Malcolm Hawker gripped the phone, his temples throbbing, jaw taut with anger. After a deep breath, he continued.

"What do you mean, Roberts has vanished? When was the last communication with him?"

There was a brief pause. The caller was clearly choosing his words with care.

"Our last communication with Mr Roberts was two hours ago. His situation was somewhat dire, sir."

"And? Spit it out, man. We haven't got all night."

"Well, sir. According to Roberts, his entire team was neutralised. He is now working alone."

Hawker was starting to feel his temper rise once again, the caller proving to be negligent at his job. He made a mental note to rectify said problem once he got back to London.

"Really? And I'm hearing about this now? What is the status report on the Marines and the incursion itself? Am I to assume Mr Roberts has entirely failed to contain the situation?"

"I'm afraid that seems to be the case. We tried to reach him thirty minutes ago, but alas, we had no success."

"Bloody marvellous. I don't suppose there's been any word from the surveillance team that went missing? Or have they been wiped out too?"

"It would appear likely, sir. We've had nothing but static from them."

"Oh, dear, how sad, but not entirely surprising, given the ineptitude I seem to be surrounded by. And tell me, did the delightful Mr Roberts have anything else of note to say?"

"Yes, he did, sir. He requested immediate containment of the area, and that his intent was to follow the Reservists and terminate them. We have to presume he has been successful in at least that one regard, given his experience. But sir, with regards to his request—the board refused. They are extremely uneasy regarding that course of action unless absolutely necessary. They trust you won't let it come to that. I'm sure you understand."

The old man slumped back in his chair and stared out of the hotel window, trying to assemble his thoughts. The panorama through the windows was filled with the bright lights of Bristol's cityscape. He took a hefty drag of his cigar then gently blew it out. The plume of smoke wafted in the air, calm, even in the face of all this. A salutary lesson. He returned the phone to his ear.

"Who do we have on standby regarding containment?"

"Nightingale, sir. But, like I said, the board are reluctant to use them. The chances of collateral damage, not to mention mass press coverage, is high. It's a course of action that could blow back on us with serious ramifications."

"To my knowledge, we have never had an incursion of such magnitude before, have we? And we have tried everything else. Ergo, in my opinion, the course of action you and the board are so dead against is in fact the only course of action available to us. Or am I incorrect?"

"Hmm, when you put it like that. But sir, at the risk of sounding belligerent, the board simply will not sanction it."

Hawker sat forward, his body tensing.

"Now listen to me, you spineless little cunt. I'm overriding the board. The decision is mine and mine alone. God knows what has been unleashed down there, or how far it could spread, and I won't take any more chances. Whatever is running around in the wilds of Somerset stays there. It cannot be allowed to break the perimeter. I want you to initiate Nightingale. Now. Give them free rein; take all necessary action to stem the tide. Do I make myself clear?"

The caller paused, his breathing quick and shallow.

"Understood, Sir Malcolm. I will issue the order right away, sir."

"How long until they are on-site?"

"Approximately fifteen minutes, sir. But I must, in good conscience, inform you that Nightingale will be using Mr Roberts' tracker chip to zero-in on the incursion. If, by some twist of fate, he isn't in the thick of it, we may very well lose our advantage. And if he is at the epicentre, he will also likely be...contained. I trust that meets with your approval? It doesn't give you pause?"

"Why would it? He's an asset, is he not? He is serving a purpose. Activate Nightingale. Call me when it's done."

He disconnected the phone and tossed it across the table. It was a total shit-show, but there was something to smile about at least: the prospect of Roberts being erased. It had been a long time coming. The man had been an irritant for a number of years, a blunt tool in need of an upgrade.

He stared out of the storm-lashed window and breathed his smoke. The rain couldn't last forever. As for Somerset, soon it would be raining fire.

CHAPTER TWENTY EIGHT

The Marine's body began to shake, his reason all but lost as he took in the scene before him. There had to be at least two hundred beasts atop the hill, with others crawling up its steep banks, ranked ten to fifteen deep, clamouring to lay eyes on their quarry. At the rear, towering in stature, a dozen or so gigantic trolls. Assembled at their flanks, squat dwarfs, their muscular forms adorned with matted fur and knotted beards. In front of them, some on all-fours, the sleek feline atrocities, eyes pools of emerald fire. Above them, and filling the sky, green lights streaking and swirling across the heavens as if elegantly dancing to some horrific symphony. He looked on, mesmerized by the sight of a thousand long-dead horses galloping across spiritual highways, their neighing akin to thunderous applause. Motionless at the front of this hellish brigade, stood the Huldra, surrounded by her contingent of undead Vikings and, at her feet, the apparition of the once-loyal Titan. The night reverberated now with chaotic shrills and whoops of simian delight.

"Are you not tired of the chase, warrior?"

Fergie swung the shotgun up and levelled it at the leader, his limbs trembling. What more could he do?

"One more step and you get blown back to hell," he growled.

She laughed then, high and clear. "What do you know of Hell, warrior? How little you comprehend, despite all you have witnessed. That place is of the Abrahamic faith, feared by mindless sheep and dishonourable cowards. It is a fairy-tale, a construct designed to enslave humanity. A weapon to crush the spirit of reason and smother man's true nature. We are far older, and wiser. We do not demand blind subjugation of our followers, they need not fall to their knees in fear. We demand only loyalty and strength. Pray to him if you will, but their false god holds no sway over us. We are of this land, the land of the north. Our blood is of snow and of ice, of steel and conquest." She took a step forward, as did Fergie.

"I won't tell you again. Back the fuck off!"

"I think not. I made you an offer in good faith. I will make my offer for a final time—join us at the Hunt and you will be honoured. Refuse, and my sons and daughters will feast upon your entrails. Whatever is left will serve us in other ways. You and that adorable child."

The horde edged forward, their raspy barks and hoots growing in intensity. Fergie stood firm, his eyes flitting from one monstrosity to another. He was damned if he'd go down without a fight.

"I've got enough friends, so fuck you and, fuck your Hunt!"

The Huldra raised her hand, summoning something forward.

"Fewer friends than you had yesterday. Who knows where the Hunt will lead tomorrow?""

Fergie was aghast to see the familiar figures of Downs and O'Hagan pushing forwards through the crowd, and there was Smudger! Brewer moved up to join them, and Collins too. Roberts appeared at the edge of the surging crowd, content to stand and watch. Each member of his squad bore the marks of their death in their flesh. Their movements slow and cumbersome, their eyes a vivid green.

"Oh, Jesus, no," he mumbled, as his comrades came to a halt. Smudger smiled at him, but there was no love nor passion behind the gesture. He extended his hand, bidding his friend welcome, his face a picture of hideous affliction.

"Long time, no see, Fergie. Ain't this a turn up for the

books, eh? Can't believe you left me to get killed by this lot. What kind of a friend does that? And after all we've been through... Look, come on mate. Forgive and forget, eh? Come and join us. No need to relive your past glories when there are vast new glories to be won. The Hunt needs warriors like you."

It was Smudger. It *was* Smudger. But there was nothing about him that Fergie recognised. This wasn't his friend; it was nothing but a phantom, picking at his guilt like a scab.

"This can't be real," he quavered. "I watched you die. It wasn't my fault!" cried Fergie, the words tumbling from his mouth.

"Oh, come on, fella, don't be so narrow-minded," O'Hagan chipped in. "Like the man said, forgive and forget. Death isn't the end, my friend. It's just the beginning. Join us. It'll be a riot." The bullet hole in his head glistened and seeped.

"It's an honour being part of the Hunt," added Downs, and Fergie suddenly realised why his head crooked so strangely. It had been reattached to his neck with vulgar stitches of hemp and rotten leather. "An honour we can all be a part of. Come to us of your own free will. It's better that way."

The ravaged figure of Roberts merely grinned up at him from the crowd, his body a nightmare vision of gaping wounds, inflicted by a thousand claws.

"Waiting for me to welcome you, Ferguson? Nah, ain't gonna happen. Don't listen to them. I want you to resist. To fight. I want to see you torn apart! It's the least you can do for me."

Fergie began to back away, his feet sinking into the sucking mud, hands shaking on the shotgun. But as he did so, another figure appeared from the crowd; a figure he didn't recognize, slim and pretty. She looked up and beckoned, but not to him.

"Mum!" cried Libby, and she ran from the safety of the building towards the woman.

"No! Libby, wait!" yelled the Marine, making a grab for the girl. "It's not her!" he cried, but she slipped from his grasp.

"Don't you fucking touch her!" he roared as he broke into a sprint.

Libby's mother smiled, bent down, and extended her arms, welcoming the young girl into her embrace.

"Oh, my darling Libby. Come here. No need to be afraid. Oh, how I've missed you," she cooed.

"Libby! Don't listen to her. It's a trick; it isn't her!"

The gathering began to swell, its mass pulsing with excitement.

Libby ran into her mother's waiting arms, eager to feel her warm embrace—But it wasn't warm at all. Her limbs were ice-cold, her skin almost translucent. Dark grey veins undulated beneath her flesh. Libby looked up to see thick rows of leather weaving through her throat and, where her mother's eyes should have been, nothing but hollow darkness. She recoiled, but the thing pulled her closer. Libby squirmed in the snake-like grip, her hand instinctively reaching into her jacket pocket. She pulled the knife free but before she could use it, the mother-creature lashed out, sending it spinning into the night. Eyes wide in terror, Libby pulled with all her strength, intuitively letting her legs go limp at the same time.

Fergie sensed the opportunity as Libby from the thing's grasp, took aim, and fired.

The creature managed to let out a hellish shriek as its head exploded, and the torso slumped to the earth. Libby scrambled backwards, her feet slipping and sliding in the mud and gore, trying to reach her friend.

He extended a hand. "Come on, Libby, don't look back!"

The horde let out a raucous scream, eager to avenge the kill. The Huldra extended her hand, though, commanding them to hold. A pair of creatures broke ranks anyway, their desire for slaughter overpowering, only to be brought down and savaged by others close by. It seemed a feeding frenzy were imminent. The only thing holding it back was the Huldra herself.

Fergie grabbed hold of Libby's hand and they turned. He managed only two steps before a bone-jarring strike to the head brought him down. He raised his head from the mud, gasping for breath, just as another blow fell. Libby shrieked long and loud.

"Perhaps you are not such a great warrior, after all!"

The Scotsman turned to see the fetid spectre of his former best friend looming over him, its face a picture of viciousness, its eyes little more than gaping wounds surrounding specks of green light.

"If you don't want to join voluntarily," it growled, "you've just got to die. Conscription's just as easy!" The spectre stomped a savage boot onto Fergie's neck, pressing him into the mud. His lungs screamed for air but he was pinned. Hi hands slapped and skidded, seeking purchase to push himself back.

Above him there was a sudden wail, quickly followed by a raspy gurgling sound. The pressure on the back of his neck fell away and he pushed up, gasping in a huge lungful of air before hacking and coughing up filth. Smudger—or the thing masquerading as him—had toppled off. Libby's vegetable knife was firmly lodged in the back of its neck. The undead soldier twitched a little then rolled to the side, and as he watched, the strange orbital light grew dull, then disappeared from its eyes.

Fergie dragged himself to his knees, his limbs on fire from the attack. He turned to address his saviour, but she was nowhere to be seen.

"Libby!" he croaked. His vision was blurred by white light and droplets of dirty water. Where was she?

"Submit, and she will live," came the Huldra's voice, distant and foreboding.

Fergie eyed the shotgun two metres away—*just one cartridge left*—then let his gaze settle on the Huldra. She'd been waiting for this; she wanted to have his full attention. Clasped in the Huldra's grip, Libby stood motionless, blue eyes wide in terror. The beast gave a sad little smile and gently held her fingernails to the young girl's throat.

"No, wait!" bellowed the Marine as he staggered to his feet, his hands to the heavens to show he was unarmed.

"I'll do whatever you want, just leave her be! She's just a kid."

"Anything?"

He took another step forward, the creatures doing the same, their claws primed. He lowered his head, his subjugation all but complete.

"Yes. Anything," he sighed.

"Then come to me, warrior, of your own free will"

Fergie edged forward, his eyes never leaving the terrified girl. He winked at her, his mouth forcing a smile.

"It's OK, Libby. Don't be scared, it will all be over soon. You trust me, don't you?"

Again, the throng began to cackle, the air electrified with throaty growls of excitement.

"A wise choice, warrior," the Huldra smirked as the embattled Marine stopped before her.

"Now, on your knees," she hissed, to the jeering of her minions.

The man gazed down at Libby, her face awash with tears, and he nodded slowly.

He returned his attention to the Huldra. "I have your word she will not be harmed?"

The she-beast nodded.

Fergie dropped to his knees and lowered his head.

"Then do as you will," he whispered solemnly, resigned to his course.

The Huldra cast Libby to one side, her tiny body coming to rest in a puddle. She wiped her hair from her face and propped herself up on scuffed and bleeding elbows sobbing quietly. The Huldra bent down, her claws resting either side of the Marine's head.

"Don't you hurt him!" Libby screamed.

The Huldra shot her a menacing glare, green eyes glinting.

"Silence, child. Fear not, your turn is coming." She tightened her grip and breathed into Fergie's ear.

"I bid you welcome to the Hunt, warrior...." And her fingers dug into his flesh.".... for all eternity!"

Fergie saw his opening and acted with dizzying speed, stabbing upwards. The Huldra screamed, a deafening sound reverberating across the storm-battered Tor, as the ancient spearhead slammed through her jaw, crossed her gaping mouth and pierced her skull from below. Fergie rose to his feet, mountainous in his fury, the momentum forcing the tip through the top of her head.

Her grip slackened and fell away as he pulled the blade free. Then, with an explosive show of brute strength, he slammed it home, straight into her heart. Around them, the creatures howled as swirling green phantoms burrowed through flesh and earth, then shot weeping through the sky.

Libby ran to Fergie, who was lost in his frenzy. The Huldra's body fell to the floor, green mist leaking from the wounds, but Fergie did not let up. He lashed out again, her body nothing more to him than a slab of meat. He only ceased his onslaught when, vines erupted from ground about her, their edges barbed like blackest night. He staggered back and looked on in horror as they began to twine around the fallen monster's limbs, snapping bone as they tugged her down into the muck.

A devastating clap of thunder seemed to rock the very earth they stood on, and the clouds began to whirl. Hand-in-hand, Fergie and Libby backed away from the site, and the ground beneath their feet split wide open. The Huldra's body tumbled down, half-devoured, half dragged by the snake-like tendrils. With an ear-piercing shriek, the remnants of the horde charged forward, their leash now removed.

Fergie snatched at Libby's hand, and they ran towards the tower, its blackened shape offering some semblance of sanctuary. Fergie caught sight of the shotgun, and managed to bend down and scoop it up without breaking his stride.

His limbs screamed for fresh oxygen and a moment of rest, but they dared not pause; The creatures were right at their heels. The Scotsman hefted the shotgun and opened up on the nearest vision of teeth and barbarity, spattering its brains on the walls.

"Stay behind me!" he bellowed as he swung the empty shotgun like a club. There was nowhere else to go, nothing else they could do, so he kept on swinging.

And then came the sound. A sound Fergie hadn't heard in many years; a sound he never thought he would hear again. It was distant, yet gaining ground. A deep thumping, edged with a mechanical drone that could be felt in the pit of his stomach. He buried Libby's head into his chest and looked up at the tower's walls, to its vibrating brickwork, flurries of masonry and mortar breaking free to litter the floor. He eyed the myriad creatures, their bodies now eerily still at the doorways, their eyes to the heavens in a state of awe and confusion. Fergie spun around and flung his body over Libby's, his weight taking them both to the floor the Apache helicopter shattered the darkness, its downwash screaming through the building and out through the open doorways.

"Don't move!" he shouted, his voice struggling to be heard above the chopper's engines.

Above them, the helicopter banked hard, its powerful turbines whining as it turned, then increasing as it gained speed. Outside, there was a bestial roar as the creatures turned their attention to the new threat. None of them had seen anything like it, of course. The cars and vans in the town below were clear analogues of carts and wains but this—it must have seemed like some vast mechanical dragon to them. Some began to flee, the darkness swallowing them whole, others stood their ground, defiant, their eyes cast heavenwards. Then, amid the primal cacophony, a new, devastation shook them: the distinctive thump of the chopper's M230 chain gun.

With a deafening roar, the pilot opened up, and the horde scattered under the impact of his 30mm rounds. The impact sent geysers of earth across the sodden landscape. Tower stonework shattered as the heavy-calibre bullets pierced its ancient walls, reducing the upper levels to rubble. At the base, Fergie clung on, screaming with Libby as the world crumbled around them.

Beyond the tower, those taking direct hits virtually exploded under the devastating attack. There was no let-up; the chime of spent cases a symphony of righteous retribution.

Then the pitch of the engine changed. Slowed.

Fergie shook his body free, dust and stone fragments falling away as he stood. He quickly checked on Libby. Her small frame was curled up in a ball, but she was breathing, and thankfully seemed uninjured. Satisfied, he made his way to the doorway, stepping past bodies, revelling in this most-welcome of massacres. Looking out, he saw dozen, hundreds of their tormentors' lifeless corpses strewn across the hilltop. Yet, a considerable number remained. Some had not been caught by the helicopter's initial attack. Other slowly regained their bravery, skulking back from the shadows as the helicopter began to rise.

There could only be one reason to do so with the job half-done. He swore, turned on his heels and fled. He didn't bother to explain things to Libby; time was a luxury neither of them had. He just grabbed her and ran through the rear door, swinging her up into his arms. The steep edge of the Tor loomed fast but he kept on running. As he threw himself and Libby over the edge, tumbling and rolling through the blackened void, the chopper dropped its payload, a cylindrical mass the size and approximate shape of a whiskey barrel. The legends of the horde recall this as the dragon's breath. The humans describe it as Napalm.

CHAPTER TWENTY NINE

Behind them, the bomb landed centre mass, a direct hit on the Wild Hunters. The resulting explosion was truly staggering: a surge of heat and fire that engulfed the Tor, lighting up the sky for miles as the burning chemicals washed over beast, corpse and hellish devotee.

Fergie tucked in his extremities as they fell, his world reduced to flashes of sky and fire, rock and earth as the remnants of the blast flew past him. The air was red hot, burning his lungs, and the acrid stench of petro-chemicals saturated his senses.

He couldn't slow his descent; neither did he have any idea of the state of Libby. He held his breath and closed his eyes as his body was battered remorselessly by rocks and branches. It was then he came to a sudden stop, his head slamming off a large rock, his leg wedged against a tree. He tried to move, but his limbs were unresponsive.

Fergie coughed a large globule of blood which landed on his chin, and let out a gargled chuckle. His chest screamed as his lungs expanded beneath his broken ribs. His body was shutting down, succumbing to his unseen injuries. As he sank into blackness he saw the clouds tinged with flickers of fire. It was beautiful.

CHAPTER THIRTY

Fergie took a final drag of his roll-up and stubbed it out. The ashtray overflowed with butts. He'd been here before, many times now. He winced as a pain radiated under his chest, his ribs throbbing.

The battered Marine studied the two people across the table. The smartly-dressed woman remained silent; the man shifted uncomfortably and adjusted his tie. Fergie smiled inwardly, knowing full well he had unsettled the minion. The woman, on the other hand, was a different matter. He tried to read her body language but he had to admit she was a tough one. She gave nothing away.

The room itself was barren save the metal table, the chair he sat upon, and the two stools his would-be interrogators now perched on. It had no windows nor any other discernible features, not even a clock. A small surveillance camera was mounted in the corner, next to a compact security alarm. His every move was being watched.

Days, weeks, months? In truth, he had no idea how long he had been held there, wherever 'there' was. The last things he remembered were some brief flashes from a helicopter ride and waking up in some sterile hospital ward, the only patient. He'd drifted in and out of consciousness while muted voices floated around him. He smirked at the man then returned his attention to the brains of the outfit.

"Look, let's just cut the crap and get to the part where you tell me what you want, eh? I have rights. This isn't some back-water shit-hole where you get to waterboard me. This is England, and I'm a serving soldier. Save yourselves the aggravation and let me walk, because if you don't, I'm going to kick up such a shitstorm, the only post you guys will be manning will be some dingy data-pooling office in the bloody Arctic!"

The woman said nothing to this. Fergie had to admit he was curious. She could be an instructor from the Special Forces Escape and Evasion course, he mused, possibly seconded from the infamous 14 Intelligence branch. The women from that unit were renowned for their steely resolve and feared far more than the men. Something about being demeaned by a woman just stung more. Fergie had seen many a hard man fall to such circumstances. He eyed his captors coldly.

"Aye, fine. Carry on playing your games, but you know what? After what me and my lads went through, you lot should be handing out bloody medals, not locking me up.!"

He huffed under his breath.

"Why aren't you out there investigating? See for yourselves. The bodies, the wreckage, those fucking creatures blown to pieces, scattered across the Somerset levels, thanks to us. I know you guys love all the cloak-and-dagger shite, but I'm pretty sure that not even you lot could cover up something that bloody big. And as for napalming a tourist attraction, well...."

The Scotsman drained the last dregs of coffee from his paper cup, screwed it up, and tossed it across the table. The man flinched as he did so. The woman adjusted her posture and leant forward, her blue eyes glinting coldly, belying her smile.

"You seem to think we represent the government, Mr Ferguson. I don't recall either of us stating as much. You have no rights here."

Fergie slumped back in his chair, raised a middle finger, and grinned. The woman leaned back and reached below her stool, retrieving a bulky manilla file. She gently rested it on the table and flipped it open.

"Lance Corporal William Ferguson, date of birth 18th March 1991. No siblings, mother dies when you are seven and your father leaves soon after, never to be seen again. Raised by your estranged aunt in Glasgow, no doubt in some grotty tenement hovel. Juvenile years plagued with truancy, petty criminality and then you take the next step. After a couple of years acting as a general thug for organised crime, you join Her Majesty's Royal Marines..." she glanced across at a note. "Aged nineteen. Despite a— shall we say, *turbulent* upbringing, you excel during training and sail through with flying colours. Two tours in Afghanistan, two more in Iraq, numerous attachments to combined SPEC-OPS. Highly rated at sniper/counter-sniper operations. You go for SBS selection but drop out due to a shoulder injury and subsequently lose your bottle. Dear, dear. You decide to jack it all in, only to sign up with the reserves one year later. Loves: Arctic warfare training, not to mention, long romantic walks in the countryside. Loathes: Brussels sprouts and has a deep-seated hatred for Manchester United."

She stared at him and smiled once again.

"How's that for investigating, Mr Ferguson?"

Fergie clapped his hands in mock appreciation..

"Bravo. Now that was a top-notch performance. Am I supposed to be impressed? A thirteen-year-old with a phone would be able to check my social media accounts and snag most of that. Now, like I said before, what the hell do you want? No more games. I'm tired and I can't be arsed anymore. Either charge me or release me, it's as simple as that."

The male let out an exaggerated cough.

"My name is Dominic Willets, and this," he said, gesturing to the woman, "is Ms Rebecca Cohen."

"Is this the part where I'm supposed to jump with joy? Am I on the tele? Are you guys famous? A comedy duo, maybe?"

"If only it were that trivial, Mr Ferguson, or so simple. Ms Cohen and I would have far more fun, and you certainly wouldn't be sat here. You would be languishing in Colchester Military Prison, telling your far-fetched stories about 'demons' or 'trolls' to anyone who'd listen. And you would be found guilty of murder, dereliction of duty, terrorism, and quite possibly treason."

Fergie remained silent. *Who the hell are these people?*

"No pithy quip? No smartarse comeback? It is thanks to us—and extremely lucky for you, Mr Ferguson—that you find yourself here instead. We rescued you, we patched you up, and now here you sit. You even have your foul little cigarettes. No guards, no prison bars. Just the three of us having a nice cosy chat. You are still a free man, Mr Ferguson. In a manner of speaking, anyway. Why do you think that is?"

Fergie snatched up his tobacco tin, and rolled up a trio of cigarettes.

"OK, I'll play. You want something from me. Something more than my fairy stories. I'm pretty certain it's not because you enjoy my sparkling personality."

Cohen leaned forward.

"Do you believe in the supernatural, Mr Ferguson? I mean, after what you have experienced, you would have to say yes, would you not? But before that, would you have staked your flag and announced to the world that there are things outside of science, beyond our comprehension? How would you have reacted if someone had relayed to you the events you so recently witnessed? Would you have scoffed and dismissed them as mad, or would you have given them credence? Please answer honestly, Mr Ferguson. Your future rests upon it."

"I don't need any kind of validation for what I saw. I lived it. But, if someone else had told me? Yeah, I'd have called bullshit. Of course I would. But what does it matter now? I killed it; she's gone. End of." Fergie took a drag of his cigarette.

"I'm afraid that's where you are wrong," Willets stated.

"Eh? What the fuck do you mean by that? I'm telling you we killed it. I stabbed it with that magical spearhead and then you guys blew it back to the stone age."

Cohen slowly shook her head.

"I'm afraid not, William. You didn't kill it; you merely survived to tell the tale. That's it. You needn't feel bad—we are all extremely impressed by your grit, but you present us with a unique problem."

"Oh, aye? The kind of problem you send men like Roberts to solve? Let me guess—I know too much. Am I warm?"

"To be frank, you are pretty much the only living witness to The Wild Hunt..."

Willets interrupted her.

"Now, here's where things get really exciting. Look, Ferguson, we are not the government, nor do we answer to them—their participation would be disruptive at best. You see, we serve a higher purpose. Off the radar. We are, in fact, a privately-financed group who investigate—and, if the need arises, terminate—esoteric threats to our species."

Fergie stared at him, confused by the direction the conversation had taken. Willets continued, oblivious to all but his private enthusiasm.

"We receive no medals, no kudos, just the chance to live one more day without some otherworldly horror having us as a midday snack."

The Scotsman held eye contact, desperately trying to make sense of this, looking for any sign of a joke. He could find none. Either they were telling the truth or they had the best damn poker faces he had ever seen.

"Let's just say, for argument's sake, that I'm buying into this whole 'superhero' bullshit; that you really aren't some bunch of power-hungry of toffs. This top-secret monster club got a name?"

"Why, of course we do, Mr Ferguson. We are called the Solstice Initiative and our mandate is simple. We are the very last line of defence against the horrors that modern science is unable to explain. As with anything pertaining to the occult, the vast majority of the population don't believe, and simply go on with their lives unawares; some people do believe, and choose to capitulate. This is regrettable, not to say dangerous. We, on the other hand, choose to fight back. Hard. Some use magic, some use modern tools, but we like to use both. Believe it or not, we have found from personal experience that a bullet can do just as much damage as a well-placed curse—or magical spear, for that matter— depending on the enemy we face. But I'm sure you are well aware of that."

Fergie was stunned.

"Back the fuck up. You mean to say there are more things like that out there?"

Cohen nodded.

"Mr Ferguson, what you have witnessed is just the tip of the iceberg. There are threats to our world that you could not possibly imagine. Threats which, should the truth get out, would send the world into anarchy. I am not exaggerating when I say that the simple knowledge would cause society as we know it to tumble into the abyss. Our very survival hangs but by the thinnest of threads every second of every day. We, and our antecedents are the only reason it hasn't so far."

"So, what? you want to lock me up then, so I don't blurt my story to the papers? You're wasting your time with this whole clandestine scare-tactics routine. No fucker'd believe me anyway."

"If we thought you posed a threat, William, we would simply have you removed. Permanently. There are plenty of men like your Mr Roberts, I'm sure."

Cohen was a cold bitch. He was starting to like her.

"Aye, is that so? So why am I still breathing then, Ms Cohen?" The door opened and two new arrivals entered the room. Fergie's heart skipped to see the little girl, but it was the old man next to her who spoke.

"Because I see potential in you, Mr Ferguson," the newcomer said with some gravitas. "And because you took care of my granddaughter."

The man was in his late sixties. Not fat, but of solid build. His greying hair was trimmed high and tight, paired with a well-manicured beard.

"My name is Sir Malcolm Hawker. I am, what you might call 'the big cheese' around here."

Libby edged forward and smiled.

"Hi, Fergie," she said. "Nice to see you again, I'm glad you are on the mend." The words seemed right, but the way she said them seemed strangely devoid of emotion. Her eyes held amusement though. A smugness almost.

"Granddaughter? Didn't see that one coming."

"Not many do, Mr Ferguson. She's a special girl. Her mother, my daughter—God rest her soul—was a member of our collective. She was an asset, and a very good one at that. Some might describe her as a psychic, a conduit to other realms. Sensitive, certainly. She was a firm defender of everything that we, in this room, hold dear. Sad to say, we became estranged. She made the decision to keep our relationship purely professional, which I respected. In fact, we hadn't spoken in years, though I made it my mission to keep an eye on young Libby here. It would appear that she has inherited her mother's gift. In fact, we believe that Libby is the very reason you are here today—alive, that is. The Huldra knew of young Libby's gift and was actively seeking her out—at least that is what we theorise: The Wild Hunt is not merely wanton slaughter; they have a quarry in mind, a use for those rare humans with a psychic bent. Doubtless one of the reasons that heinous woman toyed with you for so long, probing and testing. You were really quite lucky to have met dear Libby, otherwise I am sure your colleagues would have died much sooner."

The girl smiled up at her grandfather with something like pride in her pretty green eyes.

"Of course, Libby's father knew of my daughter's affiliations and hated the fact that his own daughter had inherited such talents. He considered her inhuman, can you believe it? My daughter and I were in accord about one thing at least: we were glad when he left. Good job really, I never did like him. As far as I am concerned, he was a lesser species. A bit like you and your men, really—I mean no offence by the way. I am merely stating a biological fact."

"You really are pompous wanker, ain't ya?" spat Fergie.

Hawker's smile faded. "I beg your pardon?"

"Did I stutter?"

"No need for such unpleasantries, Mr Ferguson. We have much to discuss still. Let's keep it civilised, shall we?"

"Civilised? You call my lads a lesser fucking species and expect us to become best fucking pals? You ever speak of my boys like that again, I'm gonna paint the walls with yer brains, ya wee cunt."

Hawker shook his head, smiling tightly. "Ah, the famous Scottish banter. Are you quite finished?"

"So, what happens now, Gramps? You already sent that English prick out to kill us, not to mention all the civilians caught in the crossfire. Gonna finish the job? Dump ma body in some shallow grave?"

Hawker began to laugh and, to his outrage, Libby joined in. That hurt more than anything. Fergie could feel his blood boiling. He glared at each of them in turn.

"What's so fucking funny?" he hissed.

Hawker stepped forward and slapped his hand on Fergie's shoulder.

"I apologise. We forget sometimes how impulsive and emotional the ill-informed can be. Yes, I am responsible, Mr Ferguson, as far as Mr Roberts is concerned at least, but I cannot pretend empathy for your plight. I gave the orders, and I would do so again were a similar situation to occur. These are the stakes we face and the choices that must be made. In the grand scheme of things, it doesn't really matter, so long as the living outnumber the dead. The world is a dark place, William, shrouded in shadow—to which sacrifices must be made." Hawker's condescending smile stretched the width of his face. He waved his hand dismissively. "Rest assured, there are no rainbows and glitter in our world. But enough of such things; you needn't be worried, my dear fellow. It is not our intention to kill you. I thought I had made that plain. You have potential. And I wanted to thank you, in person, for taking such good care of my Libby. She is the heir to my organisation. My legacy. And she has nothing but praise for you. Apparently you did an outstanding job protecting her from all that nasty business."

Fergie clenched his fists as Hawker slid his hand beneath his suit jacket and pulled free a 9mm Sig Saur pistol. The Marine tensed and prepared to move, but then hesitated as the old man placed the weapon on the table and took a step backwards.

"What you see before you is a choice. A choice to do the right thing, to put all that training of yours to good use and to serve a higher purpose. However, before you decide, you should bear in mind any loved ones, friends or even associates, that may be put in 'danger' should your decision be unwise. I ask you, with the utmost respect, whether you are a wolf or a sheep, Mr Ferguson?"

"I'm a wolf." snapped Fergie. "Look at ma teeth, you arrogant prick."

Hawker leaned forward once again, ignoring the outburst. He tapped the gun gently with his finger and pushed it across the table towards the Marine.

"No preamble, waffle or hesitation. I appreciate that. In that case, I want to offer you this. It is a gift, a golden ticket to greater things. What you do with said gift is your business. Although, I must warn you, the offer is time-sensitive. We need a solid replacement for Mr Roberts."

Fergie snatched up the pistol and ejected the magazine. To his surprise, it was loaded. He replaced the mag and worked the slide.

Hawker let out a hearty laugh.

"Let's put this business behind us then, and move forward. What say you, Mr Ferguson? Do you want the job? Will you keep your remaining friends safe from the 'nastiness' lurking in the shadows?"

Fergie gripped the pistol tighter, his fingers aching. He knew what he wanted to do, but he was pinned. Willets and Cohen sat silently, watching. His gaze settled on Libby, nestled in between Hawker and the table, peering up at him intently. She'd seemed to be such a sweet girl, but there was something darker there now, beneath the surface. A cold stone settled in his stomach as he looked into her eyes. Her *green* eyes.

"Just do what Grandad says, Fergie. You don't want Smudger's little girl to lose her mother as well, do you?"

Fergie's movement was a blur. He hefted the pistol, levelled the barrel and pulled the trigger.

Hawker's body dropped to the floor, the wall behind him splattered with brains. Cohen managed a single scream before she took a round to the face, her body slumping onto the table. Two more blasts, deafening, and Willets tumbled from his stool, half his skull gone.

Libby shrieked as Fergie aimed at her. She backed away, reaching for the door handle.

"Fergie, No, I—"

The Scotsman didn't hesitate. Three rounds centre mass, two more to the head in quick succession. Her body was thrown against the door with the impact. He watched as she slid to the floor, green mist and pooled blood expanding around her.

The room was suddenly plunged into a red haze as the alarm was triggered, the bulb in the corner flashing brightly; from outside the room came the sound of raised voices and running footsteps.

Fergie tossed the pistol on the table and slumped into his chair, a fresh roll-up between his lips.

"How's that for rainbows and fucking glitter?" he whispered as the door came crashing inwards.

THANK YOU FOR READING

Thank you for taking the time to read this book. We sincerely hope that you enjoyed the story and appreciate your letting us try to entertain you. We realise that your time is valuable, and without the continuing support of people such as yourself, we would not be able to do what we do.

As a thank you, we would like to offer you a free ebook from our range, in return for you signing up to our mailing list. We will never share your details with anyone and will only contact you to let you know about new releases.

You can sign up on our website

http://www.horrifictales.co.uk

If you enjoyed this book, then please consider leaving a short review on Amazon, Goodreads or anywhere else that you, as a reader, visit to learn about new books. One of the most important parts about how well a book sells is how many positive reviews it has, so if you can spare a little more of your valuable time to share the experience with others, even if its just a line or two, then we would really appreciate it.

Thanks, and see you next time!

THE HORRIFIC TALES PUBLISHING TEAM

ABOUT THE AUTHOR

Former nightclub Bouncer and unwaveringly proud Heathen who loves nothing more than expanding people's minds with Pagan related Non-Fiction or blowing people's brains out with fast-paced, gut-wrenching Horror / Thrillers.

Harley lover & avid movie nerd, Stuart has never followed the crowd but instead carved his own path and danced to his own tune.

Since his early years, Stuart found escapism in both the written word and the silver screen. A massive fan of 80's Action / Horror movies such as The Thing, Aliens, Predator & Die Hard and literary heroes such as Shaun Hutson, Clive Barker. Richard Layman and Brian Lumley, Stuart endeavours to bring an unapologetic cinematic eye to his fiction in the hopes of rekindling his childhood sense of wonder, all while blowing through vast amounts of ammunition down his local shooting range.

He currently resides in Glastonbury, UK with his long-suffering wife and man-eating Shih-Poo dog "Poppy" where he owns a kick-ass Viking / Asatru shop, fiercely named "Wyrdraven."

ALSO FROM HORRIFIC TALES PUBLISHING

High Moor by Graeme Reynolds

High Moor 2: Moonstruck by Graeme Reynolds

High Moor 3: Blood Moon by Graeme Reynolds

Of A Feather by Ken Goldman

Angel Manor by Chantal Noordeloos

Doll Manor by Chantal Noordeloos

Bottled Abyss by Benjamin Kane Ethridge

Lucky's Girl by William Holloway

The Immortal Body by William Holloway

Song of the Death God by William Holloway

Wasteland Gods by Jonathan Woodrow

Dead Shift by John Llewellyn Probert

The Grieving Stones by Gary McMahon

The Rot by Paul Kane

Deadside Revolution by Terry Grimwood

High Cross by Paul Melhuish

Rage of Cthulhu by Gary Fry

The House of Frozen Screams by Thana Niveau

Leaders of the Pack: A Werewolf Anthology

Scavenger Summer by Steven Savile

And Cannot Come Again by Simon Bestwick

A Song for the End by Kit Power

http://www.horrifictales.co.uk

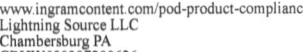